The Book of Maggie Bradstreet

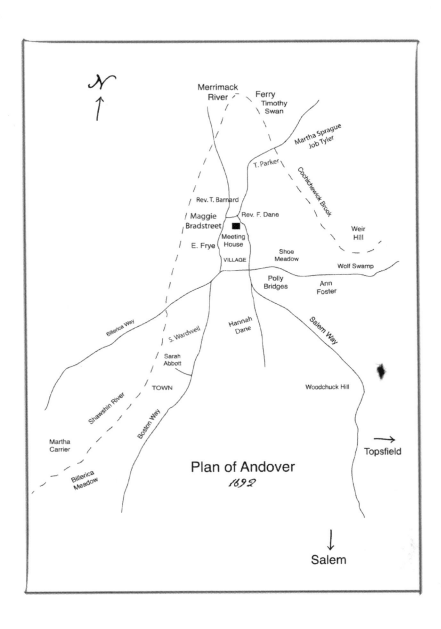

N

Merrimack
River
Ferry
Timothy
Swan

Martha Sprague
Job Tyler

T. Parker

Cochichewick Brook

Rev. T. Barnard

Maggie
Bradstreet

Rev. F. Dane

Weir
Hill

E. Frye

Meeting
House

VILLAGE

Shoe
Meadow

Wolf Swamp

Polly
Bridges

Ann
Foster

Billerica Way

S. Wardwell

Hannah
Dane

Salem Way

Sarah
Abbott

Shawshin River

TOWN

Woodchuck Hill

Martha
Carrier

Boston Way

Topsfield

Billerica
Meadow

Plan of Andover
1692

Salem

The Book *of* MAGGIE BRADSTREET

Gretchen Gibbs

Glenmere
Press

This is a work of fiction, and is produced from the author's imagination. People,
places and events mentioned, while based on historical records from 1692 in
Andover, MA, are used in a fictional manner.

ISBN: 978-0-9852948-0-9

Author photograph: Diane Pell Photographer, 845.986.1268
Plan of Andover: Adapted from Plan of Andover, Copyright © 1992 by
The Historical Societies of Andover and North Andover, used by permission
Cover design: Gini Hamilton www.ginihamilton.com
Interior Design: Winged Books info@wingedbooks.com

Printed in the US

In memory of my parents, and their parents,
and theirs, back through time.

Acknowledgements

It's a cliché, but I couldn't have written this book without my writing group, which at the time consisted of Fran Cox, Gini Hamilton, Carole Howard, Lois Karlin, and Anita Page. What a remarkable group of women, both as friends and writers, and how lucky I've been to have their support and suggestions. Special thanks to Lois, who helped with Maggie even before the writing group took form, and who designed the book. Gini designed the cover in her impressive style. Other friends and family have read the manuscript and helped me on my way, but the writing group was a constant presence. I also want to thank Rebecca McClanahan, who read an early version of the manuscript and taught me much of what I know about writing.

Thanks to my mother, whose research into our ancestors I didn't appreciate at the time, and to my father, who could always tell a good story.

Preface

This is a work of fiction about historical events. Almost all the characters in the narrative really existed, but I have had to invent their personalities and some of what happened.

With the exception of Secret Way and Mossy Green, all the places mentioned, like Weir Hill, Woodchuck Hill, and Shoe Meadow, can be found on the map in the frontispiece, adapted from a map prepared by the Historical Societies of Andover and North Andover.

The afterword will clarify which events in the story happened exactly as I've described and which involve my invention. I am not a historian, and I apologize for any errors of fact or interpretation.

Gretchen Gibbs,
March, 2012

Twenty Fourth of May, 1692

I begin here an account which is my very own, which no other eye shall see, of my life here on the Boston Way, in the Village of Andover, in the Town of Andover, in the County of Essex, in the Colony of Massachusetts Bay, in the New World. Mother gave me this book, from England, with dark green leather binding and so many blank pages, on the occasion of my thirteenth birthday, three months ago. I like to touch my book's soft cover, but this is the first time I have written in it.

We were sitting at the evening meal tonight, Father and Mother at one end and Dudley and I at the other. I like this time of year, when the days are lengthening and we can eat without candles. Dudley and I were as usual trying to spoon the best pieces of the chicken stew off our shared trencher before the other should get them, while appearing mannerly so that we should not be sent from the table.

There was only the clunk of the spoons upon the wooden trenchers when Mother said, "Maggie, why have you not written in your fine book? You were instructed to write in it each day after breakfast."

She went on at length about how fortunate I am to have been taught to read and write beyond the horn book. I am the only girl in Andover who can read, other than Sarah Abbot, who reads ever so slowly (and is also fat), and my friend Hannah Dane. I wish that my best friend Polly Bridges could read, but she cannot, only a few words and write her name.

I replied, "I know that I am fortunate, Mother, but after I have fed the chickens and gathered the eggs and fed Tobey and Molly and the sheep and ground the samp and heated the water and set out the table and eaten my breakfast and cleaned the trenchers, then thinking of something to write seems another chore."

Mother said, "Impudent child! Thank the Lord that you have eggs to gather and a pig to feed." She said that I must recall Father's mother (whom I never knew), and remember how her poems and writing instructed her children.

I bowed my head and said that I feared that while Grandmother was most accomplished, yet I am not, and words do not come easily to my pen.

Dudley said, "I could take the book. Words come easily to me."

"They do indeed," I murmured.

Mother said, "Yes, if Maggie does not use the book, then Dudley shall have it."

I looked up at Mother, my face flushed.

Father spoke then.

"No, the book was given to Maggie. Tis hers. Maggie, the book shall be your very own. You may write in it as you please and neither I nor Mother shall open it."

I bowed my head again to hide my smile of pleasure. Mother looked at Father with a frown.

Dudley said that perhaps he could read my book, as he could help me improve my writing. He knows that my hand is cramped and makes spots of the ink. He did not dare to say that he would help me with my spelling, since my spelling is especially fine.

"And Dudley also shall not read your book," Father said.

I trust Father intended his vow, but I shall try him by first writing of something that he would not like me to know, and see whether there are consequences.

What I know is that there are Witches. Of course, all know that there are Witches, and in these times there are many Witches. People talk of little else than what is happening in Salem, though it lies twelve miles away. Dudley and I are not allowed to talk of Witches outside the house, but we cannot be forbidden to listen to others, and I am an excellent listener. Dudley says that I am a gossip, but I heed him not.

When I was a young child, I feared Witches lurked in each dark corner of my room. Sleep came hard, as every small sound became an Evil Presence that could steal my soul. The first times I heard the Witches scurrying round my bed, I screamed. Mother came running, and when I told her, she said I must not scream as it woke the family and there was nothing to fear. The next few times I felt the Presence, I screamed regardless, I could not help it, but Mother came no more. After that, each night I pulled my mattress close to Dudley's, however he complained, and when the Witches came, I lay there silent, hoping they would go for Dudley, and shivering till sleep came.

As I became older, the Witches of the night went away. I played dolls with Polly or Hannah or Sarah and there was often Witchery. Sarah bewitched her doll, and used her hand to make it twitch and carry on with fainting and spells. I never allowed Elizabeth to become bewitched. As I write, I realize that I have not played with Elizabeth for years, yet I still love her dearly. I think she is the finest doll I have ever seen, as she came from England and has a painted face with blue eyes and yellow hair.

I wish I had blue eyes and yellow hair. Tis not just that Dudley should be the light-haired one, like my mother, while I am plain brown in hair and eyes like my father. Blue eyes are wasted upon Dudley. Mother says that before Annie died she had blue eyes and hair like wisps of straw colored silk. I do not recall Annie, but I can recall Mother's grief at her passing.

I have gone away from what I wished to write. Writing is easier than I thought, but the words stray away from my intentions like sheep in the Commons when they are not watched.

What I wished to write, what I know that perhaps even Father and Mother do not know, is there are Witches here, in Andover! I know someone who is a Witch!

Yesterday Sarah told me in secret that Goody Carrier is a Witch. Goody Carrier brought the pox with her when she and her family came to town. She was accused then, but not arrested. Many died, Sarah says, but not Goody Carrier or her husband or sons, so that is a sign that she was a Witch to be able to save them. Now it has been found that Goody Carrier murdered Captain Osgood's wife and daughter! Tis especially sad to think of Captain Osgood's family murdered, as the Captain is a gentle man with a soft voice, which one does not expect in a soldier. I had thought they died of the pox, but I must misremember.

How strange! I always thought Goody Carrier was ill-natured, but I did not know that she was a Witch. Mother says that Goody Carrier is too plain spoken. I wonder if that is a sign of being a Witch.

Twenty fifth of May

Today Uncle John came to fetch Dudley and me to his farm where we pushed beans down into the corn hills. The late frost had killed the beans that Uncle John had planted before. It was hard work and Sarah would think it unmaidenly and tease me for it, especially the way my petticoat grew black and dirty.

I enjoy being outside, and would rather plant than sew. It was a lovely day, neither hot nor cool, with the sun shining brightly upon the white hawthorn blossoms. Sarah says that Witches can turn themselves into hawthorn trees.

At our meal, Uncle John gave me the larger piece of rhubarb pie, with a wink, saying that I had planted more than Dudley. Dudley had been carrying on about his studies at Reverend Dane's, about how he will pass his examinations and go to Harvard to become a minister in the fall, even though he is but fifteen. How tiresome to be a minister and have to be good all the time. Dudley is not really so good, particularly not to me, but merely thinks he is. He is always dropping phrases into the conversation that others do not know so that they will think him learned. He is silly, not learned. His eyebrows rise up on his forehead when he lectures at us. Polly has told me that he reminds her of an owl, though his eyes are blue and his eyebrows thin and fair.

When Uncle John brought us home, Father sent Dudley and me up to the loft to sleep, and asked Uncle to stay a while. I lay as still as I could so I could hear them. Father said that he had been to the jail in Salem, which is full of Witches, and that it is damp, airless, and cold. The Witches have no blankets. Today one of them died.

If they are Witches, why do they feel the damp, and why did one die of it? Why did not the Devil deliver them?

Tis strange that Father sounded like he felt pity for the Witches. I must talk with him alone.

When I see my friends' fathers, I know that I am fortunate. Father lets me talk with him about many things. Polly's father is too often in the tavern, Hannah's father is stern, and Sarah's father is self-important.

Twenty seventh of May

When we rose this morning, Stacy was in the front room sitting in Father's chair bent over with his hand upon his huge back and his eyes all squinted up.

"Oh," he said, "My back is hurting mightily."

Stacy said that he had hurt it hauling water to the house. I haul the water often, though not in so large a bucket as his, and it has never hurt my back. Mother said sharply that he must leave Father's chair at once, go to his own house, lie all day in the dark and not set foot in the tavern on any account. Mother has no patience for illness in anyone.

After he had gone, Mother complained that he is always sick, or hurting somewhere, and that he does the least work about the house of all of us. Ruth has told me that Stacy gives himself airs as his father was White and only his mother was Black. Stacy will not talk with her as she is all Black.

I think that Ruth likes it not that she must share her little house in the back of our yard with Stacy, who is half her age and twice her size and not half so agreeable. She must cook and care for him as though he were her kin, and he is not. Ruth seems so tiny next to him. She is no taller than I am, and she told me that in her last years she has grown smaller! Can that be?

Father said that he would haul the wood for the kitchen fire since Stacy could not. I sprang up to help. It was still cool, though the sun was already sharp. I had planned my question so that Father would not know that I had eavesdropped. I said that Sarah had told me a Witch had died in the Salem jail.

"Should I feel pity for her?" I asked.

He said I need not pity a Witch. However, being a Witch and being accused of being a Witch were different. Those accused must be tried to see if they were Witches. She who died had not yet been tried, and could have been innocent. He reminded me of the time that I was sent to bed without supper for forgetting to gather the eggs, and it happened that Dudley had stolen the eggs to give to a tinker for a new whistle. I said that showed only that I was often blamed while Dudley went unpunished for his misdeeds.

He said not to think about myself, but to think like a justice, like him, about what is fair and within the law. He began to talk about the way that trials are held, and how there are different rules for witches' trials. I did not understand most of what he said. I found myself noting instead the way the morning light reflected off Father's high forehead, and I saw that his hair is thinning. I do not want Father to grow old.

6

This morning Mother scolded Ruth for running short of salt without telling her, and then she sent me to Peters' store to fetch some. I love to take time from chores to go to the store, even though it is only a short way down the Billerica Way. The store is set to one side of the tavern, and folk gather there.

When I went in, Eunice Frye, the worst of the gossips, was nodding her head fiercely as she spoke of someone. She stopped abruptly when she saw me. I wished I had heard what she was saying. There is always something to be learned from Eunice.

She said to me, as though I were a wicked girl, "Does your mother know you are here?"

Her breath is bad, and she speaks close to my face, so it is an advantage to keep my head bowed politely. I wish she did not live next to us, as I always feel her notice upon me. I said, with my head down,

"I have been sent for salt, Goody Frye."

In my mind she is never Goody Frye, but always Eunice Frye. I know that I must call all married women Goodwoman to speak to them, yet I need not in my mind. Eunice is a detestable name, and it fits her fine.

As I paid for my salt, the conversation continued, about who is sick and whether there might be witchcraft behind it. I heard mention of Timothy, and I think it must be Timothy Swan, who is most ill for someone of his age, twenty-nine.

Eunice Frye said, "I have seen a black cat hanging about old Ann Foster's house, mewing and howling, and it spat at me."

Someone murmured something I could not hear. Black cats are not remarkable, yet of course any animal may be a familiar of a Witch.

As I left, Sarah was walking up the Billerica Road. She was out of breath, and at first I thought it was from walking, since her bulk makes it hard for her. Then I saw she was excited. She pulled at my arm, and said she had been coming to find me.

She whispered loudly in my ear, still gasping between the words, "Tomorrow Goody Carrier will be arrested as a Witch!"

I could think of nothing to say.

"Would it not be an astonishing thing to see!" she said.

The thought of it made me gasp myself, and I pulled her away from Peters' up the road a piece. We sat underneath the big maple tree that stands near the Johnsons' house, while Sarah gained her breath. At first it was make believe that we should go to see the arrest, and then as we talked we made a plan. I wished to invite Hannah and Polly as well, but Sarah does not like Polly. She says that Polly is a poor Puritan, and I think what she means is that Polly is poor. I argued, as I like Polly so much, but Sarah said four of us would be too noticeable, and in the end I agreed to invite only Hannah. I must tell Mother tonight that I wish to go tomorrow to Sarah's house to knit.

I stopped on the way home to tell Hannah of our plan. Her mother came to the door, and said Hannah was waxing the furniture, so she could not come out. I asked if I could help her, and went into the front room. I love the smell of turpentine and wax. Hannah was bending over the table, her thin hands rubbing the mixture in long strokes into the wood with a rag. I did not help, but watched only, as she was almost finished. Her face had that tight, determined look she gets, and the two arches of her dark hair in its widow's peak escaped her bonnet. She is always pushing her hair back in, but she could not then as her hands were covered with wax. Hannah's mother was working on the sideboard, and when she finished, she went back into the kitchen.

At once I began to whisper to Hannah. She was startled at the news about Goody Carrier, as I had been before. When I whispered our plan to see her arrested, her pale face turned paler and she shook her head violently. She whispered that her mother and grandfather would be sorely vexed. I wish Hannah were not so timid, and that her grandfather was not Reverend Dane.

I said, "No one shall know. You may never have another chance to see a Witch!"

In the end, her mother came from the kitchen and asked what we were whispering about. I said that Hannah wished to come knit with Sarah and me tomorrow but was reluctant to ask her.

Hannah gave me an astounded look, and Hannah's mother said, "Of course she may go." I said I would meet her tomorrow at the cross-roads of the Billerica and Boston Ways.

That night at dinner, I asked permission to speak, and then to go to Sarah's with Hannah to knit. Mother said I might go if I promised to attend more closely to the stockings I am knitting. They are most badly shaped, and I fear no one will want to wear them.

Then Mother looked down at her plate and blushing slightly said, "What think you, my husband, of expanding the back of our house? We could have a proper dining room like the Abbots, and not have to eat in the front room like ordinary folk. Then the front room could be a parlor."

Father raised objections, like the cost and having the kitchen in the middle of the house, because of the heat in summer. Mother said the back room would become the kitchen, and the middle room the dining room. We could use the middle room for other purposes as well, and Father would like it as he could keep his books there instead of crowded about the front room. In the end Father said "Perhaps."

I was trying to pay attention to the talk. I do not care that much for a finer house, or for house goods of any sort, though I do love the blue bowl from England which holds the walnuts in the winter, the apples in the fall and now holds nothing so that I can see the blue like deep water upon the bottom.

My mind kept going back to what would happen tomorrow.

I was not sure Hannah would come to meet me at the cross-roads, but she was there before me. She that said she came because she did not want to tell her mother of my deceit, yet her step was lively and her eyes were bright.

It was cool when we set out, headed for the Town. I had worn my heavy dark green petticoat over my chemise, as I thought the green would blend in with trees and bushes so that we would be less likely to be noticed. I was carrying my stocking to knit, and Hannah was carrying the first square for an afghan, in a shade of gray I do not admire.

We took the track that goes straight to Abbot's, but we detoured by Peters' store, to hear what they were saying. There were folk outside and we could hear them talk of something that had happened yesterday in Salem. Then someone said that a small bird had entered their house and one of the family had begun to cough and spit. Someone went "Ooh," and someone muttered, "Witchcraft."

Then I heard Eunice Frye say, "No better than she ought to be," as we passed. I think she spoke of me.

When we reached Sarah's in the Town, we told her mother that we were going for a walk, and we set out further south for Goody Carrier's house. Once we left Abbott's, none of us knew for certain how to travel the back ways, as there are no other houses along them, and none of us go that way. We argued twice as to whether we should take the right fork or the left. Sarah said we must listen to her as she lived closest and knew the paths best, but she led us astray once. It was a long way, several miles at least. The track kept getting narrower, with small trees and brush on either side, until we had to walk single file. Sarah was gasping, Hannah said her feet hurt, and I was sweating in my heavy green petticoat when at last we saw the smoke of a house ahead.

10

As we got closer still, Hannah began to complain that now we had arrived we would have to turn back. There was the Carrier's house stuck out close to the river, with only a few willow trees about it. There was no place for us to hide. Then I noticed another grove of willow trees also on the river, about a hundred feet from the house. As we headed toward them, a dog at the house began to bark. We feared that someone would come to the door and see us, but none did.

The sun was straight up in the sky when we arrived. Although everything was quiet, the smoke in the chimney told us they were at home. There was nothing to look at, only the weathered boards of the house, and the pig rooting in the yard. The roof needed mending, and there was much clutter in the yard with old barrels and broken tools lying about.

We strove to be as quiet as the house. It was hard not to speak for so long. Hannah said to imagine that we were at the Sabbath service. Then while we were feeling solemn, the bull frogs began so loud that we started to giggle. The mosquitoes were coming up from the river fiercely, and we were slapping each other and trying not to make noise with the slapping, and then we would start giggling again. We wished we had brought something to eat.

Nothing happened for the longest time. Finally the door opened and Richard came out, long dark hair falling over his eyes. We hushed. He was only coming to throw a pail of water from the kitchen upon the garden. He went in again in a moment. I had thought Richard to be Dudley's age but he looked older. I seldom see anyone from the Carrier family, as they do not come to Sabbath meetings.

Hannah was whispering that Sarah and I had brought her on a fool's errand, that her feet hurt grievously, her arms were covered with bites, and that she wanted to go home, when we heard the sound of a carriage lumbering along on the narrow track, having a hard time of it. We could hear the branches thwacking at the carriage. Then we saw the black horses and the black carriage, and then the Constable's crest on the side of the carriage. We moved around the trees to be sure they hid us. My breath quickened.

That carriage always makes me think that Constable Ballard is looking for me for the bad things I have done. Whenever I see him, I recall the time when we were sitting at the board and I forgot and spoke right out without asking about how Tobey had attacked a bear. Constable Ballard's tight red face grew redder as he told me I was a impudent, sinful child and would end badly.

The horses drove right up to the house. Sarah grasped my arm so hard it hurt and said, "Now we shall see."

Two men got out of the carriage. One was Constable Ballard, large and red, and the other, a short bald man in a black robe whom I did not know. Sarah whispered that he might be a Sheriff from somewhere else.

Constable Ballard was looking at his carriage, rubbing at a mark upon it, and swearing. Then the short man called to him and they went up to the house. Richard must have heard them, because he came to the door and quickly went inside again. Perhaps he was trying to bolt the door, as the men pushed on it as though there was force behind it. Finally the two men gave a shove together, the door gave way, and they entered the house.

We heard loud voices, and then a horrid screech. The hair rose on my arms. They dragged Goody Carrier, wearing an old brown petticoat, from the house. I heard the skirt rip as they pulled at her while the children were holding onto her from behind. Goody Carrier screamed and screamed, while Richard yelled, "You filthy swine, leave her be. She is no more Witch than you. God's wrath upon you!"

Sarah kept pulling at my sleeve and whispering, "I told you. I told you. See, she IS a Witch!"

When I turned to look at her, her face was swollen with excitement.

The three left in the carriage, the short man in front, and Constable Ballard and Goody Carrier, still screaming and struggling,

12

in the back. Richard shook his fist at the carriage, shouting some oath I could not make out. We could hear the other children crying from inside the house.

Hannah said she was feeling poorly, and wanted to go home. My belly was churning also.

Sarah said, "Well, she shall not murder anybody else!" Her stomach seemed unaffected.

Besides feeling sick, I was disappointed. I had thought to see Goody Carrier perform magic upon the Constable rather than struggle as any person might. Could not she have flown away, or at least caused him to double over with a stomach grippe?

I told Sarah I thought that Captain Osgood's wife and daughter had died of the pox. Sarah said that was true, but that Goody Carrier gave them the pox with the Devil's aid, and the Devil's ways are not to be fathomed.

I went home, my shoes in a sorry state, and fearful that Mother would note my long absence. I was glad to find Mother and Father so thick in talk that they did not notice me.

Father said, "A pity this has come to Andover."

Mother said, "Goody Carrier may be the only one. She has been called out as a Witch before. She is no gentlewoman, to her misfortune."

Father said, "It is not her manners only. She has come to grief over the piece of land out near Billerica Meadow. She said in public that she would stick to Benjamin Abbot like bark to a tree to prevent him taking that land."

Benjamin Abbot is Sarah's uncle. So there is trouble between Sarah's family and the Carriers. I did not know that, but I did think it was strange that Sarah knew before everyone else that Goody Carrier was a Witch.

I am confused by the way Father and Mother spoke, because it is not Witchcraft to have argued with Sarah's uncle. Did Goody Carrier murder Captain Osgood's family or not? She must be a Witch, or she would not have been arrested. I wish I could ask Father what he and Mother meant, but I cannot think of a way to do so without him knowing I was eavesdropping.

When Mother checked my knitting today, she was vexed that I had done so little, and that I cannot hold the pattern better. I wanted to go out to talk to Hannah or Polly, but she required me to stay in all day and do chores.

Mother did not chide me for my journal, however, so I shall continue, and shall write with even less caution. I shall have to be careful about Dudley, however, as he is watching me curiously this moment as I write. Regardless of what Father said, I would not be surprised if he felt it was his duty to read anything I wrote.

I shall hide my book, but there are no good hiding places in the house, and in the barn it could get wet.

Yesterday after we left Sarah and continued on our walk home, Hannah sat down on the stone wall along the way. First she pushed the wings of her hair back under her bonnet. Then she took off the long narrow shoes of oxblood leather that I have often envied. She began to rub her thumb into the arch of her sore red feet. She showed me the blister on her little toe, and how high arched her feet are, so that they pain her when she walks a distance.

I sat with her for a time, feeling impatient, and tried to remember what I like about her. Hannah is mightily good, and I try to admire that. She is also clever, and thinks of interesting things. She told me that "Andover" is the same as "and over" and one can say, "Andover Andover again." But it is always Hannah who tires first, or who develops a megrim, or whose feet hurt, or whose back aches. I fear she has little spirit.

To distract her from her sore feet, I told her that I am writing in my book. Hannah said she would like to get a book to write in also. I have not told Polly about the book in case she would be envious since she cannot read or write. I try not to show Polly my things, or to talk about them, as envy is a sin and it is not good, Mother says, to put temptation in the way of others. Polly has so little. It is sad to go into her house, with only a dirt floor, no windows, no upper story, and all seven of them in the one room. I do admire the hinges upon the door and windows, and the knocker shaped like a lion's paw striking against the door, things her father has most cleverly worked at the smithy. It must be hard without servants like Ruth and Stacy. Polly only has two chemises, one bonnet and three petticoats. Her winter gray petticoat is very ragged.

Hannah and I talked about what we had seen. I said that I had been disappointed that Goody Carrier had seemed so ordinary, and Hannah said that there was no accounting for the Devil's ways. I also told Hannah that I did not like the way Sarah took delight in Goody Carrier's plight, even though she is a Witch. Hannah pressed her lips together at me and said,

"You must be charitable toward Sarah."

That is the price of having a minister for a grandfather. If only Hannah were plainer spoken.

I am perplexed about what people say and do not say. Sometimes I feel I am the only one who has thoughts they cannot speak. At other times I wonder if all folk have such thoughts, and if all do, why all do not speak them. Is plain speaking indeed a sign of the Devil's work? I like writing here, regardless.

After I left Hannah, I thought as I have before that Polly is my favorite friend. Polly is always plain spoken. She never gets angry at me, and has a merry laugh with her freckled face and wide smile. She has many good ideas for things to do, like going into the forest, which no one is supposed to do because of Indians and wild animals. We take Tobey and he is such a good dog that I know he would protect us from anything. (Now I will see if my parents keep their word; if Mother finds out I have gone to the forest, I will never hear the end.)

Second of June

Today was the Sabbath. What is best about the Sabbath is that we live right across the way from the Meeting House, so we do not have to walk a long way or ask Stacy to harness Hector to the carriage. When the guns are fired for the far-away folk, I enjoy looking out the front window so that I may see the carriages and farm carts pull up. And then when the gong sounds, I watch in earnest to see people walk in and what may be new about them. Today I saw that Eunice Frye, who only wears black because she is a widow, had a new petticoat of shiny black silk that swayed when she walked. She enjoys display of herself though she would deny it. Sarah Abbot had taken one of her mother's petticoats, in russet, and had it reworked for her. Nothing looks good on her because of her large form, and russet does not suit her blonde hair and pale complexion.

As I was walking in, Henry Chandler sat in the stocks. Father had mentioned that Henry had been drunk and rowdy in the town and that the case had come before him. I did not look at Henry, as I never look at anyone in the stocks—it could be me there instead. Mother is always saying I shall end in the stocks.

I enjoy walking into Meeting House last, when all eyes note our passage down the aisle to the front seats, Father and Dudley first, veering to the right, and Mother and I following, going to our benches on the left. Of course by walking in at the end, the commons was even muddier than usual, and Mother was angered by my muddy shoes, saying I was not careful enough.

When one walks into the Meeting House with all those people, there is a foul odor, worse in the summer. Polly says the smell is worse if you must sit by her grandfather, Goodman Tyler, who does not believe in cleansing the body at any time. Services seemed especially long, though they were as ever, merely two and a half hours in the morning and then two hours and a half in the afternoon after eating. As always, Reverend Dane spoke in the morning, and Reverend Barnard in the afternoon. I knew they would speak today of Witches, so I thought it would be less tiresome than usual, but I found it hard to listen.

I do not know how a man can speak for two and a half hours. Of course, in most parishes, it is the same minister who speaks both times, so it is even harder. I try to imagine Dudley speaking for five hours. Perhaps he would enjoy it. When Father asks him to say Grace, he does go on about it, so that often we do not get to eat until the food is cold.

Reverend Dane is always hard for me to follow, as he gets worked up, his long gray hair swaying back and forth as his head nods to mark the important points, and his large mouth forming the words ever faster and in a higher pitched tone. He spoke of Evil, and how we must root it out from our own minds so that we might see it clearly in the world about us. I tried to examine my mind for Evil, and resolved to avoid vanity and to be more charitable toward others, toward Hannah and Sarah and perhaps even Dudley.

People favor either one or the other of the Reverends, and my family favors the Reverend Dane. Father says that Reverend Barnard is not so intelligent, though he went to Harvard. He says that Reverend Barnard is nothing but a mouthpiece of the Reverend Cotton Mather from Boston, and that he has few ideas of his own. I do not know what mouthpiece means exactly. I imagine a piece of

Reverend Mather's mouth upon the pulpit, perhaps the upper lip, or the tongue.

At all events, my father is a friend of Reverend Dane, and Hannah Dane is my friend, so I try to understand the Reverend, but when I listen my mind goes round like the clouds swirling in the wind. I keep hoping that soon we shall sing a Psalm, which I enjoy more although there is no real tune since each of us starts out upon whatever note we choose. Still it is loud and joyful.

Reverend Barnard is easier to understand than Reverend Dane, though he has problems with the letter "s," and sprays on it, which I can see from my seat though Polly cannot tell from hers. Reverend Barnard spoke of how Witches are here in Andover, and how Goody Carrier is a sign that Evil has come to our town. He said that she was brought into the Salem court, and confronted with five girls, who promptly fell into the most intolerable cries and agonies as soon as she looked at them. The Reverend said that Goody Carrier was over-proud and defiant, claiming always that she was innocent. The five girls writhed about and made sounds like wolves, and when Goody Carrier was forced to touch them, they were at peace. They say the Touch Test works because the witch's touch lifts the spell, yet it seems to me the touch of a Witch could as easily make a person more possessed. At any rate, it appears Goody Carrier is truly a Witch.

I turned to look at Hannah and we exchanged a look. Reverend Barnard said that Goody Carrier was taken off to jail again, as she must be tried. Father nodded his head at that.

Reverend Barnard said that we must be more vigilant to protect our town. We are far away from our Mother Country, far even from Boston, alone in the wilderness, surrounded by heathen Indians and wild beasts with only God to protect us. We must be ever alert to the Evil around us. Satan can appear in many forms, he said. Any bird or an animal may be a Familiar of a Witch. There may be Witches everywhere.

18

I know that these things are most important, and I should listen closely. I found, nonetheless, that my mind wandered shamelessly. Since there is no decoration in the meeting house save the Eye of God painted upon the pulpit, and since we are seated in the front, I see that Eye upon me ever. I tried to pay heed, yet soon after the Reverend Barnard began to speak I noted that his head is round as a pumpkin which has lain in the field on its side. That is, although his head is round, his face is very flat, even his nose hardly protruding. I also found myself waiting for the next "s" and watching where his spit would land.

I also, even more sinfully, and disregarding my determination of the morning to avoid vanity, thought of how my own blue petticoat is more handsome than Hannah's green or Sarah's russet, though their colors are sadder than my own. I do not like sad colors, although people of right mind like them better. I like bright colors, and would wish to have a petticoat that was as blue as the sky, and with it to wear a chemise as yellow as the sun. I was admiring the blueness of my skirt, which is like the blue of the sky on a cloudy day.

I then noticed a mouse peeking out from one of the holes in the wall. I started, as I do not like mice, and then I thought, What if that mouse is an apparition of Satan? What if that mouse is a Familiar of a Witch who is sitting in this Meeting House?

I was so strongly frightened by this thought that I turned around on the bench to look at everyone in the house. Eunice Frye frowned at me, Constable Ballard's red face turned redder, Hannah sitting there quietly smiled at me, Sarah was looking at her russet petticoat as she stroked it, Polly was looking out the window and Job Tyler crossed his eyes at me so I turned back around. None of these did I think could be Witches.

But what if there was a Witch in the room? Perhaps it was a Witch who made the service tiresome, and led me into vanity, although God knows I am prone to vanity at any time.

I did seem particularly sinful. Surely it was amiss of me to find Reverend Barnard's sermon so tiresome when nobody else seemed to.

If you see animals around a person, it can mean that person is possessed by Satan. How do you know? Birds get in the house, there are always mice, I go everywhere with Tobey.

According to the Reverend Barnard, there are other Witches in Andover. That is the most troubling thing, not to know where evil is, and who might be a Witch, and what animal might be a Familiar, and how they might trick you into evil.

Fourth of June

Today I did the following:

Got up at dawn, said my prayers, dressed and washed my face.

Fetched the eggs from the coop and fed Tobey and the chickens and the pig.

Helped Ruth make the corn mush for breakfast. We were low on samp, and I had to pound and pound until my arms ached. I wish Annie had lived, so that she could be the youngest child and have to pound the corn. Ruth has taught me a song to sing while pounding which helps, though she tells me I must sing it only under my breath as it is a dancing song. It has many verses, but after each one sings,

"Juba this, Juba that; Juba skin a yellow cat; Juba, Juba!"

I am not sure who Juba is, though from the way Ruth shushes me when I forget and sing loud I fear he might be the Devil.

Helped Ruth wash the trenchers after breakfast.

Gathered wood to build the fire to heat the water in the huge copper bucket for the clothes washing. Thank God washing comes but once a month. My arms ached again with the lifting and the pounding. The chemises and shirts are not so bad, but petticoats are so heavy to lift when they are wet.

Last, Ruth did the chemises that had blood stains, Mother's and mine. Ruth is better at getting the stains out than I. She has some secret herb that she rubs on the clothes. She will not show me what it is, saying if I know too much about herbs people will think I am a Witch. I told her that Polly and her mother and aunt know much about herbs, and they are of a certainty not Witches. She gave me an odd look.

Spread the clothes to dry upon the bushes in the back. It is better washing clothes in June than January, when they must be draped about the house.

Helped Ruth prepare the midday meal. Father did not come home as he knew we washed the clothes. We ate only more samp.

Helped Ruth wash the trenchers.

Took Dudley's cape to be mended. He tore it playing with Tobey, but I am the one who must take it to be mended. It must be rewoven so I was told to take it to the Reverend Barnard. It seems odd that Reverend Barnard should be employing weavers in his home, but Sarah Abbot says he must make extra money as the amount for the parish is divided between both ministers. It seems more fit for a minister to have a school, like Reverend Dane. Sarah says that the Reverend Barnard wants Reverend Dane to retire, and that he would not have come to our parish except that he thought he would be the sole minister. Then Reverend Dane would not retire, even though many think he is too old to be a minister.

Worked on my sampler, which has gone grievously awry.

Helped collect the clothes from where they dried. My new blue petticoat faded sorely in the wash. Now it is truly a sad color.

Helped Ruth prepare the stew for the dinner.

Gathered early peas from the garden.

Shelled the peas.

Plucked a chicken. (Stacy killed it for us—that is the worst.)
Gathered wood for the fire.
Knit on my stocking.
Wrote this in my book.

Fifth of June

Having noted all I did yesterday, this morning after breakfast I charged Mother with it. I listed it to her from memory, as I did not want to read to her about the rhyme that Ruth taught me. Then I said,

"Why should I have to work so hard when we have Stacy and Ruth?"

Mother said, "What an ungrateful heart you have! God shall punish you. Stay in the loft this morning and see if you like that better."

Mother's forehead creased as it so often does when she speaks to me. I do not make her happy.

Then Father came back from the Meeting House as he had forgotten a paper he needed. I heard her tell Father,

"We have not yet broken her will. Tis your fault. You put notions in her head."

Father sighed and said, "What notions? I treat her only as my parents treated us as children."

Mother said, sharply, "Your parents were as soft as pudding."

Father said, "Tis your misfortune that your own were hard as granite."

And then there was silence, and he said in a kinder tone,

"Maggie will grow up fine. I know you think of Annie often. Had she lived, it might be different for you."

Mother began to cry and they stopped talking. I know they wish to break my will, but I hope it will hold out for a time.

I n spite of being vexed with me, today Mother allowed me to take Tobey and to go with Polly and her mother and aunt to gather watercress, as it is a useful activity.

Usually I walk south along the Salem Way to visit Polly at her house. We like to watch her father work, heating iron on the forge till it is so hot it glows like how I imagine rubies.

Polly's father turns the iron into amazing shapes and useful things. It is more pleasant to watch him in the winter as the fire is so hot our faces grow red. Even in the winter he sometimes takes off his shirt, so that his huge muscles jump as he brings the hammer down upon the red iron. I like to see his body. He is the only man I have seen without his shirt except for Dudley, who is thinner than I am. I have seen men swimming in the Shawshin, but only from afar.

When Polly's father is working, I like also to look at his scars, as he cannot notice me looking. They are most strange, one of them like a bird on his neck. He has had several accidents with the fire when he was into the drink. Polly says he is not going to the tavern now.

Today I did not walk toward Polly, but she and her mother and aunt met me at the Meeting House, and we walked north on Haverhill Way toward the Cochichewick Brook. I like to say Cochichewick. It is an Indian name, and there is a place along the brook where Polly and I have found many arrow heads. It has been seven years since anyone from Andover has been killed by an Indian, but I remember it even though I was only seven.

One cannot speak of Indians to Polly's mother, as her first husband was killed by one. I should love to ask her more about it, but I know I must not. I have asked Polly what she knows, but she says only that he was the first in Massachusetts to be killed in King Philip's War with the Indians. What I want to know is how it happened, was it with an arrow or a gun, was it at night or in the day, how long did

23

it take him to die and was her mother there. Polly says her mother will not speak of these things.

We were going to the property of Polly's Uncle Tyler, who lives along the brook. Goodman Tyler is always talking about his precious cress, and how he had it sent from England, and how it is his, and others cannot have it. He does let his sister, Polly's mother, and her friends pick it. Of course, cress comes back faster the more it is picked, so he is not really so generous to her. I could imagine Dudley being generous in such a way to me when we are grown. He shall probably have the finer house, as Goodman Tyler does compared to his sister, and he will let me come to pick a few vegetables that he does not want.

I enjoy going to Tyler's because I might see Job Tyler, whom I like, though he is a friend of Dudley's. I like his eyes, which are blue and still. He looks at things closely, like he is seeing them true. I would that he had dark hair to go with them, but his hair is not too different from my own, only a few shades lighter brown. I would not like Dudley to read this passage.

It was a day of warm sun, fresh breezes and flimsy white clouds, my favorite kind of day in the whole year. It rained last night, the first time in two weeks, and the road was still muddy. My shoes and Polly's bare feet were soon black – she teases me for wearing shoes in summer. Polly's mother and Miz Post went ahead. They were talking about the Reverend Barnard's sermon, and if there are more Witches in town, who they would be. Polly's mother said Eunice Frye is the wickedest person in town, and Polly's aunt said she is too fine a lady to be a Witch. Polly's aunt favors Goody Ann Foster as she stays to herself too much.

Polly and I walked behind. I enjoy watching Polly's mother and Miz Post from behind, as they are so different, Miz Post thin as a rail and Polly's mother who is not fat but has a huge back end which pushes her petticoat out back and forth, back and forth, when she walks.

24

We talked of the Sabbath sermon, and I told about Reverend Barnard's melon head. Polly said that she had spent the service watching her Grandfather Tyler to see how long it would take him to go to sleep, which was almost at once. Then she watched the Tithing Man to see how long it would take him to notice, which was quite some time. Once he saw, the Tithing Man came to tickle her Grandfather's nose with the squirrel tail on his pole. Her Grandfather started awake with a loud oath and Polly had to cover her mouth so her giggling would not be heard. Polly always makes me feel better about being a bad Puritan.

Right where the brook crosses Haverhill Way, we passed the Parker's house. I am always curious to see Thomas Parker who is Non Compos Mentis, which my Mother says is a polite way to indicate that he is not in his head. All else call him the Witless One. Tis terrible how his little sister drowned in the stream. If Annie had lived, and I had been eleven and minding her and she drowned, I think I would not have got over it either. Thomas Parker has some of his wits, but he did not grow up. None in the town fear him, but all know it is wise to avoid going near the creek in his sight, because it excites him.

Thomas Parker is the most beautiful man I have ever seen. Perhaps it is because his face is still smooth like a boy of eleven while his body has grown up into manhood. He has broad shoulders and a slim waist. His eyes are blue and fair like Job's, but his hair is black and glossy, like a crow, almost blue. He saw us, and came to meet us and politely said "Good day," which we said back. He was splitting wood, and held an enormous axe.

"You are not going to the brook," he said anxiously. "Satan lies in wait upon you at the brook."

"No," said Polly's mother.

I wonder how God regards a lie told for a good purpose. Is it still a sin? I am not sure whom to ask.

We wished Thomas good day again, and went on to the Tyler's.

Before we arrived, Polly's mother and aunt were laughing because Goodman Tyler has a new wife and her maiden name is Hussey. They call her The Hussy. I do not like her either. She has a fine figure and even on days other than the Sabbath she wears silk petticoats that swish when she walks. Polly's mother says that she dries berries and uses them to put color on her lips and cheeks! Neither Polly's mother nor Miz Post would ever wear anything but the plainest things. They have no sin of vanity as I do.

Polly's mother says that her brother should never have married the Hussy. He is besotted with her and is led into all manner of poor judgement because of her.

The Hussy had six children by her first marriage, and Goodman Tyler had six by his. Some are grown, but most are still at home. When we came to the yard, there were many children about and much noise and disorder.

Something jumped inside me when I saw Job throwing a ball in the yard with the young boys. When Job looks at me with his blue eyes, I know he sees only Dudley's small sister, however. He talks to me as though I were a child. He joked that he would make me watch all the children, as he was tired of doing it. It is Martha's task to watch the children, since she is the Hussy's oldest daughter. She had got the Hussy to send her to town for butter, and was most slow in returning.

Job said that Martha would turn her lateness around, so that her mother would think she had good reason. I worry that he fancies her, as they are not related and he is around her so much. She is handsome, with fine dark hair that will not be contained within her bonnet and with her mother's fine figure. A man could put his hands about her tiny waist. She seems a hussy like her mother, though she is but sixteen. I wonder if she puts color on her lips, as they are very red.

Job said nothing else to me other than he pet Tobey and said he was a good dog.

We approached the brook from the Tyler's house, and went some ways down from the bridge, so that we would not be seen by Thomas Parker.

"Satan lies in wait upon you," I said to Polly and we giggled.

To gather the cress, one must climb into the water, so we all took off shoes if we were wearing them and then our petticoats so that we were only wearing our chemises, and we had to hitch them up to keep them from getting wet. Miz Post looked just like her name. When Polly's mother took off her petticoats her large back end seemed even larger. I noted that the skin on her legs is curious, like the way pea soup looks before it has cooked smooth, all small bubbles, and then larger folds of liquid within the pot. I suppose it is fat upon her legs, or perhaps that is what happens when one gets older. I looked at my own legs to make sure they were still smooth, and wondered if I should ever look like that.

The water was most cold. Polly grinned at me that the rocks were not so painful for her feet because she has not worn shoes for so long. The rocks did hurt my feet, but the cold water made them lose feeling. We cut the cress with knifes, and put it in our baskets. I love the smell of cress, and ate some of what I picked, being careful that there would be enough to take home.

While we were picking, we could see Martha, with her pinched-in waist and her black hair streaming out from her bonnet down her back, returning from town, slowly, swinging her basket. We were afar, but could see her across the muddy field, though she did not see us. Thomas Parker came out to see her and was saying something we could not hear. Then the most amazing thing happened. Martha put down her basket, raised her arms over her head, and began to dance! She was taunting Thomas, laughing at him, and swaying her body back and forth in a most unseemly way. All four of us stood stock still in the brook. Right then Tobey saw a squirrel and began to bark. Martha looked up across the field, saw us, and stopped dancing. Polly's mother shouted across to her,

"What ungodliness is this?"

Martha shouted back, "I can do as I please, you old gossip and your thornback friend!" and she picked up her basket and continued on.

Polly's mother sent us home then, saying that she and Miz Post were going back to the Tyler's to talk to her brother and the Hussy. I wished ever so hard that we could come to hear what was said but we were not allowed. Polly and I walked home, my feet still wet in my shoes, and talked and talked. I never saw anything in my life like Martha's dancing. Where could she have learned that? Polly thought she might be possessed. It was wicked disrespect to call Goody Bridges a gossip and Miz Post a thornback.

It is true that Miz Post is an Old Maid, being almost thirty and unmarried. She is the only woman I know who is not married, and I would like to ask her about it but of course I cannot. Although she is a very thin woman, with a long thin face, she is not really plain. Timothy Swan, who is so sickly, courted her, but she would not have him. I would not want him either, as he is thinner even than she, and very pale, with a nose like a small onion.

I wondered what it would be like to dance like Martha. When I was in the loft that night, I put my arms up and tried to sway like she did, feeling wicked.

Seventh of June

Margaret Bradstreet Tyler. There, I thought I would just see how it looks. I am so glad to have this book and its privacy.

I waited all day yesterday to hear some word of Martha, but none came. Today was the Sabbath again, and I was sure she would be in the stocks, or at least chastised from the pulpit, yet nothing happened. She was there as always, dressed in a green petticoat that set off her dark hair and eyes, and a green ribbon woven through the bonnet.

Polly and I had only a moment to ourselves at lunch. She said that her mother had come home exceedingly vexed, but would not speak to her. We arranged that we would meet on Tuesday in our secret place. Dudley and Job were talking quietly with each other, and I wished I could have heard.

I tried to attend better today to the preaching, but made little of Reverend Dane's sermon. Reverend Barnard spoke of all the things that are going amiss in Andover, the illness of Timothy Swan and William Ballard, how Goody Allen's husband died, and then her babe was still-born, how the seed corn that so many planted in May was washed away in the storm that came the next day, how Goodman Parker's horse died and when it was cut open it had a giant hairball, how the ferry boat at Swan's Ferry was swept away and had to be rebuilt, and so on more than I can remember. He believes that these misfortunes are to be laid at the hands of Witches.

I spoke to Hannah after the service, and asked her what she thought of it. First she said the good and kind thing, as she always does. She said that Reverend Barnard was eloquent, and that she had not noted so many misfortunes. Then she stopped. Her face looked thin, against the arches of her hair. She said in a small voice,

"I was frightened. I felt he was looking right at me and saying, 'You are the Witch!'"

I said she was being a silly wench, as why would one of thirteen years be a Witch when there are so many older folk for Satan to

29

choose? Then she asked me who the Witch might be. We talked of this one and that. I said Eunice Frye had spoken of Goody Ann Foster, as she is so old with her long white hair, and how did her husband live so long? He was a hundred and six when he died. She said that she had heard talk of Goodman Samuel Wardwell, as he tells fortunes and laughs too much.

Tenth of June

I found a loose board in the wall of the loft, and I managed to lift it out. Behind it is just enough room for you! So now you are safe from Dudley as well as Mother and Father.

At dinner tonight, Dudley and I were set to eat by ourselves first, and Uncle John and the Reverend Francis Dane came to dinner with Father and Mother. We were told to go up to bed early, so I knew they would be talking of things we should not hear. Therefore I paid special care to put my mattress near the stair frame, though not so close that Dudley should remark on it. All their voices were low, though Uncle John is always louder. No matter how still I lay, I could hear little. At one point when Uncle John waxed loud, Father said,

"Keep your voice down, Brother."

That made me listen hard.

At the beginning, I heard only the clatter of pipes, and the smell of tobacco smoke came up the stairs. Then Uncle John said clearly,

"Tis the first hanging."

Father said she was a loose woman, who ran a tavern in Salem, and no one doubted that she was a Witch. There was no pity in his voice. Reverend Dane said in his high pitched voice,

"Would that were the end of it."

I did not hear what was said then, as someone's chair scratched along the floor. They went on to talk about the Reverend Barnard's sermon on Sunday, and they were most critical, evidently hearing things in it that I had not noticed.

"Putting notions into the minds of simple folks," was the phrase that I heard my Uncle John say clearly.

Reverend Dane said, "Should not our faith call forth what is best in us?"

I had hoped to hear of what should happen to Martha for her wildness. There was not a word about her, though I stayed awake it seemed forever. When dawn came my eyes were so stuck shut I could barely force them open.

Eleventh of June

Today I stole out to meet Polly at Mossy Green, telling Mother that I was walking to the smithy to take Goody Bridges extra eggs. Tobey bounded up and down beside me. After a short ways I cut into what Polly and I call Secret Way. I always wonder if I shall see Indians, since it is an old Indian trail, but I have never seen any other person at all besides Polly and me. Most of the paths through the forest are Indian trails, which you can tell because they go straight through the woods, up and down a hill taking no curves, as Indians like the shortest way and do not mind the hills. Polly's mother told us this. She knows the forest, and has showed us many things, as where to find feverfew for megrims and swellings, and goldenseal for wounds and skin troubles. We believe that even she does not know our path.

I should like to know an Indian, even though they are Evil, and Satan is a Black Man. I think Indians might be brave, though they have done much Wickedness like killing the husband of Polly's mother.

The moss is grown upon the banks of the little stream which comes forth from the Cochichewick Brook and runs behind the smithy. I got there ahead of Polly and lay there, running my fingers over the soft greenness and looking up at the clouds. They were downy, and whiter than the stuff which sits on the spindle before spinning. I thought how heaven cannot be upon the clouds regardless of what they say, as sometimes the clouds disappear entirely. Clouds seem to be my friends, though they pass so high away and seem heedless of my presence.

I saw a long black and white face, and a large pink tongue. Tobey had come to lick my face, as he knew that lying there I could not escape. He chased many squirrels, and caught none. He is a border collie, and I think he wishes that we had more than two sheep, plus of course the cow that Stacy takes to the Common each morning, and Molly the pig and Hector the horse, and ever so many chickens. There is nothing for Tobey to herd. He does not want to kill squirrels, but to herd them. Of course they will not obey.

Polly came at last, running down the path, her bonnet askew. She had a hard time getting away, as she has even more chores than I. Her mother will tell her nothing of what happened about Martha, but Polly has listened to her talk to Miz Post, much as I listen to my parents. Miz Post said that Martha is a sly one, and her mother said that Martha is a slut. Polly said that she asked, outright, what had happened when they told Goodman Tyler about his step-daughter, and she was told to mind her manners and not to say another word about what had happened. They said that she must instruct me also that I cannot tell a soul. In fact, Polly had got away by saying to her mother that she wished to come see me to so instruct me.

At the last Sabbath, Polly spoke to her Uncle Tyler and thanked him for allowing us to pick cress. He merely smiled and nodded, and so she boldly inquired after Martha's health, as she has so much labor in caring for the children. Again, he merely smiled and said she was in fine health. So what Polly thinks is that HER MOTHER HAS NOT SPOKEN to her brother about Martha at all!

We talked for an hour about how this could be. Then we decided that Polly's mother and Miz Post must have caught up with Martha before they reached the Tylers, that they charged her with her behavior, and that something she said made them fear to speak further. But what could she have said?

Twelfth of June

Today I worked for hours cross-stitching and over-stitching a large blue flower on the bottom of my sampler. I have finished the verse, which goes:

This is my Sampler
Here you see
What care my Mother
Took of me

It is the same verse as Hannah chose, though she finished hers long ago. At all events, the flower went well and I was feeling accomplished, which I seldom do in embroidery. I went to pick up the sampler and discovered I had sewn the material to my own petticoat in several places. I was so vexed that I took the sampler and pulled hard. I had thought to break the threads of the flower that attached to my skirt, but the material of the sampler gave way and ripped apart. My sampler was ruined.

Mother went into a fury, saying she knows only one other girl who has not completed her sampler, and that is Hannah Dane's small sister, much younger than I. She sent me to the loft without supper, where I am writing now. The smell of the stew of meat and greens rose up to me and made both my mouth and eyes water with hunger

33

and sorrow. I cannot make my hands hold the needle skillfully, or even the staff that holds the wool to be spun. Some girls of three can spin on the rock, yet I could not till I was ten. My hands are like large lumps of mutton, however I try.

I listened to Mother tell Father of my wickedness. Dudley snorted. Mother said that she would set me to a new sampler on the morrow.

Father said, "Tis a shame she is a girl. She has a mind, and little skill in house husbandry."

I should not have torn my sampler. I wish I could be a right model of a girl.

Mother said I was slothful and too often wicked. Dudley said I was a disgrace to the family.

Father said Dudley's opinion had not been asked, and that I was not wicked. He said they should set me to pick a new sampler verse myself.

"Let her use her mind, then, since it is what she has."

I felt easier then, that Father does not think me wicked. Perhaps the old verse, which I chose because it was so short and easy to sew, may have worked to make Mother even more vexed with me. Now I shall try to find something that expresses better what I think.

Thirteenth of June

Today I went to Father's shelf of books and I took down the book of Poems my grandmother wrote. I had a most pleasurable hour or two reading them. The verse I liked best is:

> *If ever two were one, then surely we*
> *If ever man were loved by wife, then thee*
> *If ever wife was happy in a man*
> *Compare with me, you women, if you can.*

34

It made me think of Job. I knew better than to ask Mother if I could use it. And then I found:

> *I am obnoxious to each carping tongue*
> *Who says my hand a needle better fits,*
> *A poet's pen all scorn I should thus wrong;*
> *For such despite they cast on female wits.*

I felt a surge of love toward Grandmother, who did not like needle work either. I wish I could have known her, more than through Father's comments about her.

Finally I chose these lines, the last in a long poem about not being too involved in one's possessions and other things of the world,

> *If I of heaven may have my fill,*
> *Take thou the world and all thou will.*

I thought that was appropriate for me with my vanity.

Choosing was the pleasant part; then I had to set the lines out on the cloth with flowers and trees around them. This time I chose easier flowers that are mainly cross-stitch. Mother frowned, but she said it was better to finish it in any fashion than to work on it until I am an old maid.

Sixteenth of June

Today Mother took it into her head that we should have a cake. I was sent to Peters' for honey. As I came up, several were standing about outside, Eunice Frye and Goodman Samuel Wardwell among them, she whispering, he with his loud cheerful voice, talking of someone or another's illness and who should be the cause. How strange that both of them have been mentioned as possible Witches, she for meanness and he for telling fortunes, and yet there they stood, speculating about others. Hannah was coming in as I was leaving, so I stayed to talk. I told her how I had ripped my sampler. She was aghast and then for the first time it seemed funny and we laughed and laughed.

Reverend Dane was walking up, so Hannah went into the store, saying she must not be seen by her grandfather hanging about. Reverend Dane was with his daughter, Goody Ffaulkner. I like writing Ffaulkner as it is so strange a word. Mother says that two f's at the beginning mean that she is a lady, but Sarah says that Goody Ffaulkner is not a lady but merely married someone with money, and that the daughter of the minister should not give herself such airs. Goody Ffaulkner was wearing the most comely shawl I have ever seen, rose colored, with a long fringe and worked in pink embroidery. I should love to have such a shawl, regardless of what I am writing on my sampler.

Martha Sprague came riding up fast on Goodman Tyler's horse, the one he rides rather than the one he hitches to the plow. I would like to have a horse to ride, rather than Hector who is too old to do anything but pull the carriage, and slow at that. Martha cut a fine figure upon the handsome chestnut horse, her green petticoat and her dark hair pushing out of her bonnet. Perhaps she rode too fast. As she pulled in, and Reverend Dane and Goody Ffaulkner stepped across the street, the horse shied and threw Martha right onto the road.

I ran to her, as the others did. She was not hurt, getting up quickly, though she was covered with dust. There was a trickle of blood from her elbow and dirt all over her face. Everyone came out of the store. Goodman Wardwell laughed heartily at the sight of her. Martha began to swear, words that I would not write. She said that Goody Ffaulkner, though that was not what she called her, had waved her pink shawl, which she described in ungodly terms, and startled her horse. Of course Goody Ffaulkner had done no such thing.

Reverend Dane reproved her mightily, and said she must watch herself or God would find her unworthy. She looked at him with hatred, and when he had turned away made a rude gesture toward him.

Eunice Frye was among those present, and though I could smell her breath from two yards away, for once her prim words fit perfectly,

"Pride goeth before a fall," she said.

Eighteenth of June

I have not written for a few days. Polly and I have learned no more about Martha. I have done as Polly's mother asked, and told not a soul of what happened when we went to pick cress. Polly has not been allowed out by her mother so we have not been able to talk.

Mother said I could invite Hannah and Sarah to visit, providing we practiced our reading by reciting aloud from The Pilgrim's Progress. I have read it through several times already, yet I still enjoy reading about Pilgrim and his adventures. I particularly admire the Slough of Despond, and saying those words over.

We read each in turn. I read my part clear and quickly. Hannah read hers in her voice so soft you could barely hear her. Sarah read as though she were upon the stage, slowly making out each word, and then saying it loudly. Her large body made it seem louder still. She came to the passage,

"'You dwell, said he, in the City of Destruction, the place also where I was born: I see it to be so; and, dying there, sooner or later, you will sink lower than the grave, into a place that burns with fire and brimstone.'"

She began to shiver, and threw down the book. She said that Andover might be the City of Destruction, and we began to speak again of Witches. Sarah continues to whisper that there will be more arrests, but I think she knows little. She mentioned Goodman Wardwell and his jokes and fortune telling and the black cat that was seen at old Goody Foster's.

I asked them with care about what they hear of Martha, mentioning only that I had seen her the day we went to pick the cress. Sarah says that Martha spends her time with her friends Rose and Abigail, that the three of them do nothing but laugh and carry on, and do not attend to their duties. They are all too old for us to know well, being sixteen or seventeen, and concerned with men and who shall want them in marriage, or want them perhaps even otherwise. Hannah says it is unkind to think of them in that way, but after I saw Martha dance for the Witless One, I think she might do anything.

Twenty second of June

It was a warm day in the kitchen as Ruth chopped vegetables and I shelled peas. I had recently read the Bible story about Ruth, so I asked her how she had come by her name. She told me that the name she was born with was not Ruth, but a name that sounded something like Latitia. I can not say it as she does, sounding soft and foreign and rolling out of her mouth. My parents wanted her to be baptized, and they changed her name to Ruth, as it is a good Christian name and speaks about service to others. Latitia is a wonderful thing to say, almost as good as Cochichewick or the Slough of Despond. I wonder that she does not miss her old name. I shall ask her if she would wish me to call her Latitia sometime when there are none around.

I asked Ruth where she came from, and she said the West Indies, which is a part of the New World, but many miles away. Her family came from still another place in Africa, which is even further away than England, she says. I asked her about the West Indies, and she told me about the flowers. I can hardly believe her, yet she described flowers big as trenchers that are as red as holly berries. I wonder how they would look embroidered on a sampler. She says that it is always warm, warm as it is in Andover in July. That I cannot believe as well. I think that she misses her home, as there were tears in her eyes. She said that it was only the onions she was chopping, but onions do not often make her eyes tear. She was chopping mightily, as well, with the muscles standing out upon her short brown arms.

Perhaps she believes her home was better than it is, much as some among us who have come recently from England speak of how refined, how elegant, how wondrous in every way it was. I think Dudley should like to go to England and be swell. I would like to have more lovely clothes, but I would not like to leave my friends.

Second of July

Today I was allowed to go berry picking in the forest with Polly and her family. There are even more berries at Mossy Green, but we followed Goody Bridges and acted as though we knew nothing of the forest. We started early to avoid the heat, yet in the berry patch the sun made my head spin, as it pressed upon our bent heads, with the flies buzzing about us.

I love the red berries, though they have seeds which stick in the teeth. I cannot eat enough, and have trouble getting them into the basket. I wondered if my lips were as red as the Hussy's. Tobey, who came as well, chased small animals and wanted to play.

When we returned to Polly's house, we picked two of the hollyhocks which have begun to bloom, and pretended they were young ladies from England with beautiful rose dresses for a dance. Our skirts stand out almost like that in the winter when we must wear each petticoat that we have to cut the cold, but they are not so soft and beautiful.

On the Sabbath today, as I watched the carriages come in from town, and folk walk in from the village, I noted fewer than usual. The meeting house was almost half emptied when we walked in. As we sang the Psalms, there were so few people there I was surprised to hear my own voice, sounding wavery on the high parts.

I did not understand where everyone was, and I thought a sickness had descended, but there was no talk of any. Then after the Reverend Dane had spoken of charity and its importance to our community, we had our meal. I tried to listen to find out where folk had gone, but no one spoke of it.

While we ate, others began to come in for the Reverend Barnard's service. When he spoke, the meeting house was almost full.

Reverend Barnard spoke again about Witches and the Evil in our town. He noted that we have not had rain since the end of May, that some have lost their crops, and others spend all their days carrying water from the Shawshin or the Cochichewick Brook. He says the drought is the hand of God punishing us for our sins. There were sighs when the Reverend told how Timothy Swan was in such pain, and those with him thought he was being pricked with a pin. Someone actually spoke right out and said, "Death to the Witch." I felt like the Eye of God was looking at us all, seeing some for evildoers, and I wondered who they might be. I looked about me and saw others doing the same. I saw several eyes go toward old Goody Foster and I recalled what Eunice Frye had said about the black cat. Others looked toward Goodman Wardwell. Our church does not like men who are full of jokes and stories, though I do. Of all I could see in the house, the only one I think Evil is Eunice Frye.

40

Stacy took the cow to the Commons in the morning, and did not come back, though it is just across the way. Mother was in a fury, and set out for Peters' where she thought she would find him in the tavern. It was washing day, and she left Ruth and me to do it all.

Ruth and I dressed the bushes with our chemises and shirts. Ruth puts the clothes upon the bushes any which way, but I always put them right side up and rounded about the bushes, so that if one glances fast, it looks like Father in his best shirt or Ruth in her old linen chemise. It was so hot and dry today I could feel warm wet air rise from the bushes as I put the clothes upon them.

While we each did our own work, close by the other, I asked Ruth, or Latitia, about Witches. Mother has most expressly forbid me to do so. Since the Devil is a Black Man, Black people are prone to Devilry and must not be led in the way of Wickedness. So I said only,

"What do you think of the happenings in Salem and with Goody Carrier?"

Ruth looked up from the copper bucket, and said,

"I well know that woman Tituba they keep speaking of, who lives in the house of the bewitched girls in Salem."

I was amazed! Ruth is no taller than I, bony and wrinkled, with gray crinkled hair. And yet she knows Tituba, the Witch.

Ruth said she and Tituba came from the West Indies in the same ship, though Ruth is much older. Ruth wanted to tell me only of the grievous nature of the passage, and how they had not enough to eat and drink, and how cold and wet they were, and how many had died. I said that all who came to this country, including my grandparents, had gone through such trials, and asked her more particularly about Tituba.

Ruth said that Tituba was gifted in the black arts. I asked Ruth whether she herself knew about them, and she said that she knew

41

a little—the phases of the moon, when to sow the seed, and plants and how to use them, but she says the plants are not the same here. She said she could tell fortunes, though I must not tell Mother, and I swore I would not. I asked her, knowing it was wicked, to tell my fortune, but she refused.

She said that Tituba knows all manner of things. All say it was Tituba who bewitched those Salem girls. I began to think differently about Ruth. People are not always as they seem.

Seventh of July

Today I was churning butter out by the shed when I saw Job Tyler coming. I have watched him and Dudley talk at the Sabbath and I know they speak at other times, but I had not spoken to him myself since the day we went to pick the cress. I wanted fearfully to know what the two of them would say. Before Job saw me, I carried the churn into the barn, disregarding the two mice that scurried away as I came in.

It happened as I hoped. Job knocked at the house, and both he and Dudley came into the yard. I was able to hear almost everything. I could see them through a crack in the barn, the two heads leaning toward each other, Dudley's fair, and Job's light brown, and Job's hand against his face as he spoke. When Dudley spoke, Job bit on his nails.

Job says that Martha claims to be bewitched! He heard a conversation between his father and Martha this morning. Goodman Tyler came upon Martha and her friends dancing about in a godless manner. He charged Martha with her behavior, and she claimed the Devil made her act so. She said that she found herself dancing more and more of late, and that she felt the Evil arising from the presence of several people in the community. He asked for names, and she said old Ann Foster, whom I know she does not like.

Job's father said, "When did you first feel the Devil's presence?" and she said the day that she had encountered Thomas Parker on the road home. She said she had danced in front of the Witless One, in a way entirely different from anything she had ever done before. She said there must have been a Witch nearby to have bedeviled her so, and the only ones there were Thomas Parker himself, Goody Bridges, Miz Post, Polly, and me!

I had been holding on to the stick in the butter churn, and when I heard that, I noticed there was a cramp in my hand.

As I sat so still in the shed, the two mice that had run away came back out of the corners, and they were joined by several friends. They became more fearless, running back and forth across the barn, coming nearer to the smell of the butter. I tried to kick at them to keep them away, but since I could make no noise, they were not afraid. Dudley and Job were by no means through with their conversation when one jumped at my petticoat and began scrambling upward. I screamed, which I know is not brave. Polly's mother simply reaches down, picks them up and breaks their necks. But I cannot. At all events, I was found out. Job was not so angry as Dudley, but they both said I must not tell.

Eighth of July

Today I broke five eggs, dropping the basket as I left the shed. Then I stepped on Tobey's foot, causing him to howl in pain. After Ruth let me separate the eggs for the biscuit dough, I dropped a whole yolk within the whites so that they were spoilt and Ruth had to change the recipe. I do not know what is the matter, but it has to do with Martha, and it is more than that she says she is bewitched.

43

Ruth and I made the mutton stew for our dinner together, with much fresh mint, to be served with the jellied mint we made last fall. Ruth said I must call her Ruth and not Latitia, as Mother might hear.

I have been pleading with her to tell me my fortune, and she finally agreed, looking at my palm for a long minute. Then she said,

"Your life line is not long. You shall marry and have six children."

"Whom shall I marry?"

"Nay, I have not the power to tell you that."

"Will he have blue eyes?"

"Perhaps."

The Sabbath again. Even fewer came in the morning for the Reverend Dane, who with his gray hair flying about him spoke against looking to others to explain away our own sins. He said that when the crop fails or the mallet is lost, it is easier to say, "A Witch did it," than to think of how one failed to weed the peas or was careless with the mallet. Our Psalms sounded a most thin praise to the Lord.

Many more came to listen to the Reverend Barnard in the afternoon. I listened almost the whole time with fewer than usual of my wanderings of mind. Each word spoken by either minister seemed to carry more than its meaning. Reverend Barnard went so far as to say "The ones who should be most vigilant toward Evil are the very ones who turn their heads aside from Evil." I knew he meant the Reverend Dane, and I felt Mother stiffen beside me, and people spoke right out and said "Yes" in the congregation.

Martha came only to hear the Reverend Barnard, with her friends Rose and Abigail.

Reverend Barnard spoke of the sad illness of Goody Ballard, with her strange pains and pressures. Goodman Ballard began weeping. I have never seen a man weep before, except Dudley, when he was twelve and I broke his finger with a mallet, after he tormented me wickedly. I suppose it is terrible to fear your wife should die. Goodman Ballard is so distraught he has been leaving the whole running of the mill to Constable Ballard who complains he cannot manage.

Father says it is hard for brothers in the same business. He loves Uncle John, but would not want to work with him. I know I do not like to work with Dudley.

The Reverend Barnard called a prayer meeting for Goody Ballard on Friday.

Twelfth of July

Tonight Father and Uncle John and the Reverend Dane met at the house, earlier than is their habit. They took no care that I was in the kitchen and listening to every word. Perhaps they did not think to look because there was no light in the room, and they did not think anyone would sit there quietly without light.

I am noting all that was said. I did not understand it all, but I wish to. Perhaps if I read it over it I will understand it better.

Reverend Dane began by saying that my father was the foremost citizen of the town. I suppose that is true, although I have not thought it out loud myself. The Abbotts have a finer carriage and a finer house, and people speak to the ministers with more reverence, but my father is respected in another way.

Father did not dispute it, though he said,

"It is not me, only that my father was twice governor of the colony."

Uncle John said, "He is my father also. Tis you, not I, who are

45

the magistrate and the representative from the town to the General Court."

My father said he wished that he had chosen farming like John rather than the law.

Reverend Dane said that his position gave him responsibilities, and that he must speak out more strongly. Father said that his responsibilities meant that he must weigh matters carefully before speaking out. Father said,

"Your own plain speaking has helped neither you nor Andover."

There was silence, and Father apologized. He said that he felt he had a responsibility to represent the town and the opinions of its members.

Father said that the Reverend Dane's opinions were not those of the Church. Reverend Dane said he reckoned not, but that Cotton Mather was not the Church either. I have seen Reverend Mather once when we went to a large Sabbath meeting at the Boston North Church. His voice rings out more powerfully than either Reverend Dane's or Reverend Barnard's.

Reverend Dane said that Cotton Mather had trained Reverend Barnard in his image, and that was a grievous misfortune. He said Father must speak out from his conscience, ignoring what Reverend Barnard is saying from the pulpit. It is hard to tell his feelings from his high-pitched voice, but he sounded angered.

Father said that it was a sin for a man to put his own opinion before that of Church doctrine. "There are Witches," he said, "We know that."

Reverend Dane left at last, saying, "You are not a brave man, Dudley Bradstreet."

Uncle John stayed a while longer. He said that Reverend Dane was upset, and that he has lost touch with what folk feel in the community.

Father spoke to me today. I thought I had stolen up to the loft like a mouse last night, but he saw me. He was less angry than I thought he would be. He asked me whether I were afraid of Witches. I said I was not, or at least only a little. He then asked me if I thought there were more Witches here in Andover. I said I knew not, and that Mother had forbade me to talk of it. He made a face and said he wanted to know truly what I thought.

I love Father. An ease came over me as he spoke. I said that people talk of little else, that Sarah Abbot says there are many more, and that there shall be arrests soon. He sighed, and asked me what I think myself. I thought of how Martha Sprague was calling herself bewitched, and how I knew that none of us present that day at the creek could be the Witch who bedeviled her.

I said, "There may be Witches, but there is a perplexity in discovering who they are. Any may call another a Witch, and there is no way of knowing."

He nodded and smiled, and I knew I had pleased him. He began again to tell me what he had spoken of before about the trials, and this time I attended more closely. In trials of Witches, any can make an accusation, and then it is hard to prove innocence. Spectral evidence may be used, which means that any can say,

"Goody Carrier came to me in a dream, and told me she was the Devil's handmaid," and that can be evidence. It is necessary because the Devil's work is devious, and He wreaks such grievous harm. If the Devil has sickened a person, one can not expect Him to leave a poison by the bedside with a note that he did it. The Devil cannot take the form of an innocent person, so if Goody Carrier came to me in a dream and bedeviled me then she could only be a Witch. Or at least that is the theory. Surely if you disliked someone you could make up such a dream.

I asked about the girls in Salem, and he said that they were used to identify witches. Their suffering increases in the presence of Witches, and it decreases when the Witches touch them. I asked him why the touch of a Witch should relieve them, and he said that it is supposed to undo the spells that have been cast. There was something in his tone that sounded like he did not quite believe this.

Finally, he asked me what I thought of what I had heard last night from the kitchen. I said I thought he was a most brave man. He touched my arm and said I must go help my mother.

Fifteenth of July, 1692

Today was the prayer meeting for Goody Ballard. We were gathered in the meeting house, and it was hot. The sun came in the glass windows and struck me in the eyes so that I had to shift always on the bench and pull my bonnet down. The glass windows, newly come from England, are wondrous, but they do concentrate the sunlight mightily.

The Reverend Barnard was leading us in prayers, and I was wondering where Goodman Ballard might be, and why he was not at his own wife's service, when we heard a carriage and a coachman telling the horses to stop. The door opened, and Goodman Ballard came in, looking even more pale than usual, especially beside his red-faced brother the Constable, who led in two girls of about sixteen. They were dressed in black, and they were not handsome, but they both had striking looks, one pale and with a ruched up face, and the other tall and heavy, with dark hair and carrying herself like she was a queen. They had an odd manner, like they knew not what was going on about them.

"Who among us bewitches my brother's wife?" Constable Ballard demanded, and the girls looked about them in that odd blank way, as though they were unconscious of our looks upon them and yet they were conscious of it all. The dark one reminded me of Martha Sprague, and I turned about to look at her. She and her friends sat there and for once they also were unconscious of how they looked. They stared, unaware of how their bonnets sat or the amount of hair they showed.

The pale girl was the one that riveted me. She looked as I imagine a saint must look. Thin and tense as a spring, and with a light in her contorted face. The dark girl I did not trust, but the pale girl must tell truth.

Reverend Barnard said to her, "Do not fear, Ann."

I thought of my dead sister Annie and if she would look so had she lived.

The girls stood there awkwardly and Reverend Barnard said,

"Are there Witches here among us?"

The girls began to look at us and I shrank in my seat. I know I am not a Witch but in that moment I was frightened. The pale girl's eyes stared into mine and I felt I were seeing God or his servant. They looked at all of us, one at a time. Then they began to walk up the center aisle, most slowly, looking at everyone.

They went by the Abbots without pause. They looked at Hannah's bench, and passed on. They stopped at the Tyler's bench, and I felt dizzy as they looked at Job. They looked long at his grandfather, and then passed on. On the women's side, they looked at Martha, and she looked back at them. After a pause, they went on.

Finally they reached the next to last row of benches. There sat Goody Ann Foster and her daughter and granddaughter. Goody Foster at seventy-two, with her wrinkled skin, was the oldest woman in the meeting house, and Witches are more often old women. Her husband lived till he was a hundred and six, the oldest man ever in the colonies. I was but a child when he died. I do not remember what he looked like, but he must have been as shriveled as bacon in the pan.

The dark girl pointed to Ann Foster and ran back up the aisle to the front, where she fell to the floor, mewing like a cat, and twisting about grievously. I feared her flying limbs would hit me, as I sat in the front row. The pale girl then also dropped, sighing, "She afflicts me." Her legs faced me on the floor, and they twitched up so high so that I could see them bare under her petticoat. The room was silent, other than the sound of her shoes against the wooden floor and the mewing of the dark girl. The sun had moved from my eyes to the front, and it struck the pale girl in the face, so that she did look afflicted.

Reverend Barnard spoke then to Goody Foster, commanding her that she must come forward and touch the girls. Goody Foster is so bent over with the rheumatism that she can barely move, and the pleurisy affects her wind. She pushed herself off the bench with her cane and moved up the aisle, tottering even more slowly than usual, perhaps from fear. She reached the girls in front, and Reverend Barnard had to command her again to touch them. She bent over her cane to touch the dark girl, who kept twisting away most cruelly. It took four tries, but as soon as Goody Foster's finger had reached the dark one's shoulder, the twisting stopped. Then Goody Foster bent again on her cane to touch the pale girl on the floor, and her legs fell silent.

Someone in the crowd gasped. Another cried out, "Witch!" Reverend Barnard spoke again. "Dudley Bradstreet, you must write Ann Foster's warrant." Father rose from his bench and slipped to the back of the room where he keeps the writing materials for his work. The Reverend commanded us all to leave, with Constable Ballard only to stay and attend Goody Foster before taking her to the jail in Salem.

I spoke to Hannah on the way out, who said she felt ill. I asked her where her grandfather was. She did not know.

Sixteenth of July

Dudley and I watched the dust swell up behind the Constable's black carriage after Goody Foster was taken away. When Father came back, we sat down to the board. None in the family had appetite for the dinner, though Ruth and I had put sassafras root and new marjoram from the garden into the venison stew, Stacy having shot a deer last week. Dudley asked if he could speak, and Father gave him permission. He asked whether Father thought that Ann Foster was truly a witch. He said that others thought that she had used witchcraft to keep her husband alive so long.

"I know not, Dudley," Father said, "It may be. She shall be tried. It is why we have a system of laws."

I said, self-importantly I fear, that spectral evidence made the legal system more difficult. Mother said,

"Speak when you are spoken to, Maggie."

We ate the rest of the meal in silence, though as I said, none had appetite.

Seventeenth of July

Last night's dinner was again silent. I knew Father had gone to Salem to listen to Ann Foster's examination, but he said nothing.

As we were in the loft falling asleep I spoke to Dudley. We do not usually speak to each other when we lie down, only to say good night, often in a cross manner. I asked him whether he thought Ann Foster was a Witch. He said he knew not, but he talked of his schooling with Reverend Dane, and how Reverend Dane speaks even more boldly to them than he does from the pulpit. Reverend Dane says that many ills have been done in history through belief in witchcraft, and that good Puritans have been burnt as Witches.

"He knows there are Witches, though," I ventured.

"Of course, you simpleton," he said, and in about two moments he began to snore.

I stayed awake to listen to what Father said to Mother. Father's voice was quiet but I heard him clearly.

"Ann Foster has confessed," he said. "The Devil appeared to her in the shape of a bird."

At that moment there was the scraping of a mouse in the wall. I was reminded of how the mouse frightened me in Sabbath services, and how all animals could be familiars of the Devil.

Father said Goody Foster went to covens in the wood upon a stick with Goody Carrier. How strange to think of Witches traveling upon a stick. If you happened to look up, would you see them? I have had dreams in which I floated above the trees. I hope that was not Witchcraft.

So Goody Foster is truly a Witch, or she would not have confessed! Father sounded sorrowful. I could not take my eyes away from those girls. They are only a year or so older than I. I could become Witched myself if I am not careful.

Nineteenth of July

Today Father was home from the meeting house for the midday meal of chicken stew. There was a knock at the door, and when I answered it, there stood Constable Ballard looking stern, with a strange brown parcel in his hand, like a raggedy blanket that was wrapped around some things. I thought it must smell, or that it could bite him, from how he held it out away from him.

When I brought him in, Father did not look pleased to see him. He told me to be gone, but I could hear all from the kitchen.

The constable said, "See what I have found at the Foster's."

I could hear them placing the parcel down and unwrapping it. My father made tut-tutting sounds, like when Dudley or I have done something wrong, so that I could not endure not being able to see. I stuck my head around the door quickly and with good fortune was not noticed. There seemed to be rags and feathers in the parcel, and I did not understand.

"When I asked the women what these were, both daughter and granddaughter turned color and would not answer me," he said.

I knew then that these were witching tools, to put spells on folks, and I wished I could look again to see more clearly. Perhaps there was a piece of someone's petticoat that I would know. Perhaps there was a rag of something that was Goody Ballard's, or that was mine!

He asked Father to make out warrants for the arrest of Ann's daughter and granddaughter.

Father said, "The granddaughter is but eighteen."

Constable Ballard said, "You should have seen her face."

I heard my father rustling about for the quill and paper.

Twentieth of July

Yesterday they hung five witches on Gallows Hill in Salem. Sarah said her cousins went and it was a spectacle they shall remember all their lives.

Twenty first of July

Today they arrested Goody Carrier's children, Richard and Andrew. I recollected how Richard swore and held on to his mother when we watched them arrest her. According to Sarah, the boys are braggarts and ne'er do wells. She says that Goody Carrier will not confess to save her soul, and they hope that the boys will confess and push her to it.

I spoke to Sarah at the prayer service today. I must talk with her to learn anything, as Hannah knows little. No one listens to Reverend Dane at present. He does not speak at the Thursday service, and none come to his Sabbath service save for his numerous family members and us and Uncle John. It makes me ill at ease to be there.

At Sabbath services, I spoke to Sarah again, and she told me that she heard that they had bound Richard and Andrew Carrier head to heels until the blood ran from their noses and they confessed to everything. They have admitted that their mother is a Witch, and that she made them Witches too. They did her bidding and carried on doing evils and mischief. Twas they who broke the window in Sarah's house and they who caused Reverend Barnard's cow to die.

I know not how to write of this so I will set it down any which way. Tonight at evening meal there came a knock at the door and Stacy answered it and said it was for me and Father said they must go away as I was at the board and Polly bust in pushing Stacy to one side. She was flushed and crying and her bonnet was off her head.

She said, "Oh, Maggie, they have taken my mum!"

I jumped up and ran to her and thrust my arms about her and Father said,

"Sit you down this instant."

And I would not and I shouted that Goody Bridges was not a Witch and how could he have signed her warrant and how could he have not told me what he had done, and Polly must stay with us and he must have Goody Bridges released this moment and Father told Stacy to thrust Polly out and he took the wooden spoon from the sideboard and hit me several times on my back and said I must never speak like that again and Mother said,

"You see what comes of coddling her,"

And Father said I had common friends and that I could never see Polly again.

I ran up to the loft and I cried and cried until I could not draw breath, and now I am writing in you, though all of a which way as there is no light. I know not what to do. If there were a window in the loft, I should lower myself out and run to Polly but there is none. I could go downstairs and say I was going to the privy to relieve myself but they would come after me if I did not return at once.

I shall never think the same of my father again.

Twenty ninth of July, early morning

I said nothing to Dudley when he came up last night, waiting for his taunts, but he also said nothing. We lay there on our mattresses for some time and then he said,

"Your tongue runs away with you as though you were in your cups, Maggie, but you are a good friend to Polly."

I was so astounded that I burst into tears again, in spite of fearing how Dudley would taunt me for crying. I pleaded with him through my tears to speak to Father about the wrongness of it all, and how Polly must be helped. He said he had already spoken to Father who would not hear.

He said, "I am surprised you heard not every word, as you listen to everything."

That unkindness was more like Dudley, although I allow he spoke some truth. Even while I was crying I had wished I could stop so that I could listen to what was said downstairs. Then Dudley got up, and handed me from his pocket a piece of corn bread from the meal. It had crumbled, with dusty bits around the edges, and I was not hungry, but I ate it because it was so unlike him I was amazed.

My world is turned upside down. Father, my comfort who has understood me always, has turned away from me, and Dudley has brought me a gift.

July 29, later in the morning

This morning I longed to go to Polly, but was forbidden to leave the house. Then Ruth noted that Dudley had left his Latin grammar on the sideboard when he went off to school.

"I can take it," I said.

Mother said that I could not leave the house for anything, and that Ruth must bring it to the school. Ruth glanced at me and said she had much work to do in the kitchen.

"Maggie can do that," Mother said, but Ruth said she must make meat pies. Mother sighed and said I might go if I went straight to the Reverend Dane's and back with no stops.

I have become more sinful but I will work it out later as to how to atone to God. I am comforted that Dudley understands that I must be a true friend to Polly. I have thought about it, and I realize that Dudley's change to me is because of Job. Polly is Job's cousin, and her mother is his aunt. Job must be fearfully upset about them. Job's father has done well and is a Selectman, and their horse is finer than Hector, but Job in some ways is as common as Polly. His grandfather Job who lives with them is a scoundrel who was once accused of Witchcraft himself.

Why Dudley is my friend and for how long, I am glad of it. Right now I feel more alone than ever I have in this world.

59

What I had to do was hard, as of course the Reverend Dane's is but the other side of the meeting house on the Salem Way, and should only take a few minutes to get there and back. I had to fly like the wind so Mother would not know I lied.

Tobey joined me from the yard and we ran all the way to the school, the sun already hot through the haze of morning. I left the grammar with Joseph, and ran south along the other way to Polly's. I was glad that Polly and I enjoy running so that I was not too out of breath. Tobey thought it a frolic to run so far and fast. I told him it was a serious business, but he kept prancing around in pleasure.

When I got to the smithy, there was no smoke from the chimney, and I feared they had all gone till I saw the door was open. They were there, except for Polly's father, with everything at sixes and sevens. Miz Post was taken bad, abed and still weeping. She is Goody Bridges' sister-in-law, not her sister, but I suppose it is hard for her, as Goody Bridges is all she has. I would not grieve so for Dudley. Perhaps I would grieve some. It is possible I have been uncharitable to Dudley.

Stephen and Elizabeth were at play, and Polly was carrying Mehitable about on her hip and looking in a daze. Mehitable at three is too big to carry, but she was whimpering. When Polly put her down to embrace me, Mehitable began to bellow in earnest.

"She is hungry, I set Elizabeth to pounding the samp, but I cannot keep her at it, and whenever Stephen lights the fire it goes out."

The corn meal was mostly ground, and the fire had been laid, but was unlit. It was so dark inside, even with the door open, that I praised God for our own glass windows.

I found some cider in a jug and gave it to Mehitable, who stopped crying. If Polly was herself, she would have thought of that as well. It may be that they do not give Mehitable cider because of the alcohol but I thought it would not hurt for once. I drew Polly away from the children and asked her to tell me all as I must be away at once. She said Constable Ballard had come the evening before and taken her mother away, she knew not why or what would happen, and her father had gone to Salem to discover more. I said I would also try to find out more and would meet her tomorrow morning at Mossy Green.

As I left, kicking up the dirt as I ran, I saw the dust of a coach approaching, and I drew behind a tree. It was that black coach with the black horses that has always frightened me, and now more than ever since I have seen it carry Goody Carrier away, and Ann Foster as well.

The Constable went into the smithy. I know Polly has no parcels of rags about, but I feared all the same. I ran back west and north, the shortest way, as fast as I could, coming into our yard carefully so that Mother would not see that I returned from the wrong direction.

Twenty ninth of July 29, still later

When I returned, I went to help Ruth with the pies. She had finished mixing the dough, and had let it rest, and was flattening it out upon the table with the roller. She does not allow me to mess about with the dough, as she says that wheat flour is dear, and I make the dough tough with my kneading. Polly makes all the pies for her family and Hannah has made several.

I helped Ruth cut up the rest of the meat and suet and carrots. She asked me what I had learned, and I replied nothing, other than that the Constable's carriage had come as I left. She told me that Joseph had come to the house for eggs for the Reverend Dane, and she had found out that Reverend Dane had left the school to go to see my father today at the Meeting House. Ruth learns much from Joseph since he is also Black and of an age with her. Sometimes I think he may be sweet on her, though I do not know whether people of that age have such feelings.

I asked Ruth if she had spoken to my mother about making pies so that I could go out. She made a "hmm" sound and said that she could tell how much I wanted to go. I felt less alone.

When Dudley returned from school I was waiting in front, sitting under the elm tree, shelling peas, enjoying the shade. Most of the peas have gone already, as it is so hot and dry, but there are a few, perhaps a bushel, of small ones that must be harvested and set out to dry before they wither on the vine.

I jumped up to greet him, but as I said, "Dudley," Mother emerged from the front door. Dudley and I caught each other's eyes, but it seemed Mother did not wish us to speak. She enquired about Dudley's day and he replied politely. As I began to follow them inside, she sent me back out to finish the peas. When I finally came in, Dudley was at his lessons in the back room, with Mother sitting beside him, knitting that shawl she has been at forever. I do not like the color, like the corn meal as it cooks, already looking as though it has faded.

For the first time in my life, I long to talk to Dudley. Tonight in the loft I hope to find out what is happening.

Thirtieth of July, early morning

Dudley says that it is Martha! Martha went to the Constable with her friends Rose and Abigail and she told that Goody Bridges had bewitched her. All three of the girls are carrying on like the Salem girls. Martha has taken to barking like a dog.

Job told Dudley it is because his father found Martha kissing

Thomas Parker. His father was furious, as Thomas is so demented and Martha could not marry him. How curious! I have imagined kissing Job, and it makes me feel strange and tingly, like when there is lightning all around. When I heard about Martha, I imagined kissing Thomas, and I felt strange tingles and then distaste. Thomas is most beautiful but so demented. Martha could do nothing but say she was bewitched. I might even believe that she was in truth bewitched but for what she said about it.

Because she said that it was Goody Bridges had done it to her! I know that is only because of what happened the day we went to pick cress. The idea came into her mind that day when she threatened Polly's mother.

I could hear Goody Bridges in my mind. "Two months ago she was dancing sinfully in front of him, and was she bewitched then? or simply wicked? She should be punished for a slut."

Polly's mother would never be quiet. So Martha had to say that it was Polly's mother who bewitched her.

Whether the Salem girls are Witches or not, I know that Martha Sprague is not a Witch, she is a wicked girl. I saw her look at those girls that day at the meeting house, and she was soaking it up like bread in milk. If one can mew like a cat, then another can bark like a dog! Fie on her I say!

I know not what to do. If my father knew of what happened the day we went to pick the cress then all would be simpler, but he will not speak to me. Last night at supper I was not allowed to speak on any topic.

This morning I must get to Mossy Green to meet Polly, though I know not how.

Today my wickedness increased tenfold.

I broke the fence in the yard. I lifted one of the posts off, which was hard work and tore my petticoat. I pushed the post to the side, so that the pig could get loose. I had to move her yoke around so that she could get through the opening. Then I gave her a good wallop on the rear, so she would move smartly, or at least waddle a little faster than usual. I watched her work her way south along the road. I could see her black and white pied body sharp against the dusty road for a long time. When she was out of sight, I ran into the house shouting,

"Molly escaped. We must chase her."

I then ran as fast as I could to Mossy Green to meet Polly.

If I dwelt on it, I would think I am bewitched myself to be so wicked, so I do not dwell on it. I also could dwell on how fortunate I am that no one saw my wickedness. I am not sure how they will account for the broken fence or the rip in my dress.

Polly was waiting at our place. The stream has shrunk to a trickle in the drought, the banks are dry and ugly, and there is no coolness here.

Polly had heard herself what Martha said about her mother. She said that the Constable had frightened her even more by saying that others had accused her mother. They say she is a Witch because she is so good with herbs and grasses, and last year cured little Frances Ffaulkner of the croup with bloodroot. So folk say that she could cause disease as well.

Miz Post is still in bed, and Polly is out of her head with trying to keep the children fed. Her father has taken to the drink again and is always in the tavern. None come to him for work now but go to Salem for their blacksmithing.

Polly clung to me piteously and begged me to speak again to my father. I vowed I would, but I feared it would not help. And indeed when I tried to speak of it to him this evening he would not listen.

Thirty first of July

No one caught Molly yesterday, but Joseph told Stacy when he came out from the tavern that a pig had showed up at Reverend Dane's, eating the grain that had been left out for the horse. Stacy went to get it and brought it back by its ring after some chasing. No harm done, I told myself, though we shall have to pay for the grain. I have mended my petticoat myself, and hope that Mother shall not note the rough stitches I made.

Today was the Sabbath, and again no one came to hear the Reverend Dane speak save his family and us. He spoke more boldly than ever before. He spoke of the sin of ignorance, and that those who believe in Witches commit that sin. We must look inward to our own sinfulness to see why God has punished us. I felt the weight of my past wrongs upon me, and I wondered if it could be my own sins that had hurt Polly's family.

Hannah told me afterwards that her grandfather had debated whether to deliver this sermon.

"We fear for him," she said. She also said she was sorry for Polly, though she and Polly are not friends.

In the hours between the services, as Ruth and I prepared the table in our house, I was astonished to see Grandfather walk in upon his cane. He was accompanied by a large man dressed as a preacher whom I recognized after a time, from the attentions that were placed upon him, to be Reverend Cotton Mather. I had not seen Grandfather

65

for months as his health is not good, and he does not stir from his house in Boston. It is why he had to give up being Governor, as he did not have energy to manage. Uncle John came in soon after, so a family gathering must have been planned.

Reverend Mather had a prodigious amount of curly reddish brown hair, coming off a large bare part in the center, so that it looked like two large furry animals hanging off each side of his head. I was reminded of Job and Polly's grandfather Tyler, who trained a red squirrel to eat off his bald pate. Then I saw that Reverend Mather was wearing a wig, which it is not the habit of men in Andover, but only in Boston, so that I am not used to it. He is not a handsome man, with a large nose and nothing notable in his features, but his eyes are set wide apart, which Goody Bridges says is the sign of an honest man. He spoke to Dudley, asking him his age and his intention in life. When Dudley told him that he was fifteen, and that he would go to Harvard to become a minister in the fall, he clapped him on the back and wished him well. He said,

"When I was your age, I had already been two years at Harvard. Of course, my father was President of the College!"

Reverend Mather did not speak to me. I did not expect him to, as Dudley is the boy, yet it would have been courteous. Grandfather blessed me, asked for my health, and said he had something for us he would give us later.

Mother told Dudley and me to eat quickly in the kitchen and leave. I was prepared to obey, as when Grandfather and Father talk, especially with others present, it is always of people I have never met, and the most tiresome concerns of the government, like taxes and their collection. Then Dudley said that if we listened we would be sure to hear things of interest regarding the trials, and perhaps something that could help Polly and her mother. So we did not speak again, and ate slowly, and managed to hear quite a bit before Mother came in and pushed us outdoors.

I have talked to Dudley about what was said, so that I understand it better than had I listened only by myself. They began by speaking of the drought, Uncle John claiming that with the late frost and the lack of rain, he had never seen such a poor crop. Reverend Mather said that it was a clear sign of the times, "I have never a drop of patience with a man who denies Witchcraft and the trials it places upon us."

Then they were talking of the trials, and many of the accused, including Goody Carrier.

Reverend Mather said, "Martha Carrier is a loathsome hag, and the Devil hath promised her she shall be Queen of Hell."

Remembering how she had been dragged from her house in her old brown petticoat, I wondered, as I had at the time, why if she was to be Queen of Hell she was not able to save herself, or at least her sons.

They began to talk about spectral evidence. I did not understand many things, but Dudley said that the Reverend Mather was arguing for its necessity, while Father was questioning whether it should be abandoned, as it made the legal process so difficult.

At this point Mother came and made us go outside. After the Reverend Mather left, Dudley knocked at the door to ask if we could return, as we so seldom see our Grandfather. Mother said we might, if we waited in the back room for a bit until they were finished with their Madeira and conversation. She waited with us, picking up her knitting. She began to talk of the morning sermon, not the part about Witches, but about questioning one's self and respecting others, especially one's parents. She said that times had changed so since she was a girl that she would never have thought to have an outburst like mine of two days ago, no matter if the world were ending. We divided our listening, appearing to hear Mother, but in fact trying to hear the speakers in the other room. Afterwards we talked of what we had heard, and Dudley helped me understand what was said.

First, Uncle John said, "Now he's off to see his protojay."

(Dudley says this means Reverend Mather was off to see Reverend

Barnard, and that protojay is a French word that means somebody who follows one).

Then Uncle John said, "Tell us why you came with him. Your groom could have brought you, and Mather is bound to add to the inflammatory atmosphere."

(Dudley says that inflammatory means adding fuel to the fire, that because the Reverend is a Witch hunter and a well known figure and because he's come to Andover and thinks there are Witches here, people will believe even more strongly that they should find more Witches.)

Grandfather replied that Mather would have come by himself, and he thought it better to be there to put a bit of water on the flames. Mather was not going to inflame the Bradstreets, and better for him to meet with them than others.

"He is most involved in the goings-on in Salem already," Father said. "Three of the magistrates are his close friends. I should not like him to be more involved here as well."

Grandfather said that his sons were too fearful of Mather's influence.

"The man is not far off the mark. Think you not that there are other Witches lurking about the town? Why else the drought, the rash of illness?"

Mother was telling a story of when she was a girl and she had only one toy, a doll made of corn husks, that she named Nell, and her voice wavered as she spoke of it. She had a quarrel with her little brother, who took Nell and fed her to the goat.

Father was saying the only thing I heard about Polly.

"I find myself in the middle of it, more than I wish to be," he said. "I have had to write the warrant for the mother of Maggie's friend. There is some evidence, and I know I have done the right thing, though Maggie is upset with me. I am sorry to have hurt Maggie, but I would rather she had less common friends."

I was glad to hear he was sorry, but I was angered as well. Polly is a most excellent friend, and it is not her fault that her family has no money.

Father was continuing, "Whatever happens with her friend's mother, still I am perplexed about my duty in the days to come. I know there will be other cases, Reverend Barnard and the Constable will come to me with other evidence."

Grandfather said, "Yes, doing the right thing. By whose lights, I always think. First you must do as your conscience tells you before God, but there is also the right thing for your own future. If you want to be Governor yourself someday, you must do the right thing as the people see it. Of all my sons, there are only you two left. It is a hard thing for a man to see his children die before him.

My Uncle Samuel and Uncle Simon died before I could know them. I am sure Father thought of Annie.

He went on, "Dudley, it is only you who could be governor, and I should like to see you follow me there. "

Father said, "I know not if I have the stomach for it, let alone the talent."

Mother was saying that when she went crying to her mother for Nell, her mother beat both her and her brother, her brother for the deed, and her for the tattling and too much care for things of this world. I missed some of what happened between Father and Grandfather for listening to Mother and understanding that she treats me more gently than she herself was treated. Mother stopped speaking at that point. She was bending over the sickly yellow shawl, hiding her face and her feelings from us, and we all heard Uncle John speak.

He said, "There is also the right thing to do by one's family. To stand against the public feeling in the coming days could be to risk their wrath turned against ourselves."

Mother looked up with concern, her story forgotten. Grandfather tutted and said it could not come to that for Bradstreets. He said then that he wanted to see his grandchildren, and Mother brought us in. He reached into his pockets and brought out two books, fresh from London, he said, and gave one to each of us. Dudley received a book in Latin, and I a book of George Herbert's verse.

He said, "Tis not a maidenly gift, Maggie, but your grandmother would have liked it."

I said I was sure I would like it fine, and later when I had time to look at a few of the poems, I did, though the writing is too complex, more complex than Grandmother's.

It was time for the afternoon service, and Reverend Barnard spoke especially eloquently for Reverend Mather in the congregation. I turned at several points, and noted that all watched with reverence, though a few were staring at Reverend Mather, who sat in his wig beside Grandfather and Father. They looked plain beside him.

None of the Bridges were there, so I could not speak to Polly.

I had not seen Martha since she had spoken against Goody Bridges. In my wrath at her, I wished her ugly, and I saw her in my mind blown up like a toad. It startled me how handsome she looked, more than ever, as though she had come into her kingdom. She wore the green petticoat that she always wears, that sets off her eyes. It is not new, and her chemise had a mend upon the neck, but her eyes seemed large and eager and her face was tight with happiness.

After the service, she seemed to be surrounded by her friends, though it was only Rose and Abigail. I wanted to approach her, and I felt my steps dragging. What if she were truly Witched? And even were she not, what if she accused me? She seemed to have a power pushing from her that kept me away.

I stepped close to Martha, my heart beating heavy, and said, "Why have you spoken against Goody Bridges, who is as good a woman as any in this town?"

My voice cracked in the middle. I despised myself for a coward.

She looked at me scornfully as though it were she who had the chemise edged with lace and I the one with the mended neck.

"Who are you to tell me what I can speak or not speak? I have been bewitched, and I speak only to find release." She walked away, as though I were the lowest of any.

Second of August

Father came home at midday, while I was in the kitchen helping Ruth chop cabbage to put in with the pork for the bubble and squeak. He asked me to come out to him in the front room. I was still angered with him for Polly's mother, and I walked sullenly.

His voice was severe, and his cold eyes did not look at me.

"I have sad news for you, I fear."

After yesterday when Martha frightened me, I vowed I would be braver so I looked straight at him and said,

"Nothing could be worse than you taking Polly's mother."

He spoke hotly, "Tis not I have taken Polly's mother, but the law, and all has been done lawfully. Tis you who need be minding your behavior. You are headstrong and foolish. You are not looking at what Witches are doing in this town, only looking at your own selfish feelings about your friend. Tis good to be a friend, but you are blind to her family's faults."

He said there was good evidence against Polly's mother, her use of herbs and had I ever noted that she said spells when she gave them? I had not, and I said so with spirit. And then he asked me about Polly's aunt, Miz Post.

"She has not stirred from her bed since Polly's mother was taken," I said.

He said I spoke truly and that was a sign that Miz Post was herself

71

bewitched by her sister-in-law. Without her presence Miz Post could not practice, and could do nothing. He said single women were especially prone to Witchcraft.

"Tis unkind to call them thornbacks, but there is some justice in the term," he said.

In addition there had been accusations.

"The family of Timothy Swan," he began, and I broke in,

"Timothy Swan was sweet on her, and she turned him away. You cannot take seriously anything his family says."

"There is another," he said.

I said, "Tis that Martha Sprague."

He was surprised that I knew, but tried to conceal it. He said, "That poor bedeviled girl has named her tormentors."

I wanted to cry out against Martha but I could see it was no use.

He went on, "Miz Post shall be arrested today. It is from kindness to you that I speak so that you are not surprised about it and go into another tantrum. Of course you must not tell and must stay in today until it is accomplished."

He walked away before I could ask him how Polly was supposed to deal with all the children, and with her father drinking again, though I expect he would not have thought it mattered even if he had heard. I want to write, "I hate him," over and over, though I know it is a dreadful sin, even to think it.

Polly's aunt is a good soul who has been nothing but kind to me, and she should not, not, not be taken. I wanted to go to Polly to let her know if I could, but Mother watched me every moment. They may have wondered about how Molly got loose with her yoke still on.

Later in the afternoon, Polly came to the house, but Stacy would not admit her on my father's bidding, so I screamed to her through the window that I knew, and that she was in my prayers. That was all I could do.

When Dudley returned from school, he told me about the arrest.

Job went there after school to put the house to rights, as Miz Post had to be carried out and she had knocked things about. All the children were weeping and Polly was in a bad way.

Tonight I have said many prayers for Polly, Goody Bridges, Miz Post, and also for myself to think if there is anything that I can do.

Fourth of August

It was the second night I could not fall to sleep for worry. To calm myself, I began to go through the alphabet to list things that bring me comfort and delight. It was difficult to begin, but once I started I found there were still many things.

Apples. Regardless of what is happening in town, Weir Hill soon will be red with apple trees, and the smell of apples will cover our house from the three trees in back.

Book. It is a comfort to write in you. I am writing more and more, as I am more afraid.

Clouds. I thought back to the time in June that I lay on Mossy Green waiting for Polly, and looking upward at the clouds. How much has happened since then. Clouds may still be my friends.

Dog. Tobey knows nothing of what is happening. On days when I am forbidden to go out, I play with him. We roll on the floor when no one can see us and he does his trick of shaking his paw with me as though he were a fine gentleman. His constancy makes me forget.

Elizabeth. I never play with her anymore, but I thought of her last night, and went to get her from my chest to my bed. I felt silly, but I put my arms about her and it was a comfort. I thought about Mother's doll, and her affection for it, and how Mother was a girl herself once, however hard that is to fathom.

Father is all that would come to mind, though I tried to send the thought away, and began to feel troubled all again. Then I thought of flowers. Mother's red roses, which she had sent specially from England and which she loves more than any other so that she always throws the washing water upon them, are dried and have no flowers, though perhaps they will come back next year. The Rose of Sharon which stands by the road in front of the house seems to need less water as it has come out now and is pink and beautiful. I like the Rose of Sharon, the flowers even prettier than hollyhocks, and to say the words Rose of Sharon, though I forget what Sharon is. I am sure Dudley would know, but I will not ask him, even though he is friendlier.

God, of course, though I worry about my sins.

Heaven. The same.

I could think of nothing for "I." Not I, myself, at least, I am no comfort to myself.

Job Tyler. Here my thoughts went astray and I do not remember them, but I did at last go to sleep.

Fifth of August

Mother said I might pick blueberries by myself, as they are good now and she wanted a pie. Of course I went first to Polly.

Tears rolled from Polly's eyes when she saw me. She threw her arms about me and she sobbed,

"Mother has confessed, and Auntie too! Oh what does it mean? They cannot be Witches."

I was too surprised to reply at once, but simply held her. After a time, I released her and said perhaps they had confessed to lighten their sentence. Polly said they should hang regardless.

"What shall I do?" she said. "Oh, help me, please."

I could do nothing but hold her again.

She told me Goody Carrier has been on trial and said, "You lie, I am wronged!" But her children testified against her.

Polly could not leave the children, who were fearfully dirty, especially Mehitable, and I could not return home without blueberries, so I went to Mossy Green and picked and thought about Polly and her mother. I could not be comforted by the dry hot smell of the bushes and the sweetness of the berries. I ate only a few as I had to bring home enough for the pie and must hurry because I had gone to see Polly.

Seventh of August

Today Reverend Barnard preached that the end of the world was at hand, that Reverend Mather had told him so and was preaching the same. Only by fighting the Devil with all we have can we hope to prevent it. In spite of the boredom of the service, I could feel my heart beat louder. I do not want the end of the world even should it be heaven for some. Most likely not for me.

Even so I do not see that Polly's mother and aunt could be Witches. How could they confess? I do not understand many things.

Eighth of August

Last night I dreamt I saw a large cat, the size of a small bear. It had stripes upon it like a picture I once saw of a tiger from the jungle of a distant place. It nuzzled me and spoke to me and said that I was a good girl and should go to heaven. I played with it as I would with

Tobey when there are none to see, rolling on the ground and bunking heads with it. It seemed we were at Mossy Green. Then without warning it was a Beast who swiped at me with its claw, laughed and said I was now the Devil's Child. I woke in a sweat, wondering at the dream's meaning. Was the beast a Familiar who had sucked me in and am I now a Witch? I feel no different, but if all are Witches about me whom I have known and loved, then maybe I as well.

Eighth of August, later

Today the constable arrested the other children of Goody Carrier. I have never liked Thomas, a dirty and ill-mannered boy, two years younger than I am. Sarah is but seven and she seems a lively child. It is hard to think that she could be a Witch so young even if her whole family was bedeviled.

They have also taken Elizabeth Johnson, and Reverend Dane came to the house this night in a fury. He spoke loudly, apparently not caring what Mother and I heard as we sat in the kitchen spinning.

"I have said you are not a brave man, Dudley Bradstreet, but now I think you a craven coward. You know that they think to get at me through my grandchildren. Elizabeth comes to my service each Sunday, and she holds her head up high, and that scheming Martha Sprague has spoken against her from malice only. How could you think to trust the word of that vixen over my own granddaughter?"

Father said that Martha Sprague was bedeviled, no doubt, but that they must find her tormentors. She had pointed out Elizabeth.

"That Elizabeth is your granddaughter is a misfortune, but there is nothing I can do."

Reverend Dane said no good nights and the door banged hard.

I do not think my father afraid, but I wonder what he thinks.

Father left a letter to the Salem magistrates in the large blue bowl on the sideboard where he puts the things he will take to the Meeting House. I know he did not want it to be read, but he had forgotten the red sealing wax in the pocket of his coat, and he had to go into the back room to fetch it. I read the letter hurriedly, and then ran up to the loft to ask Dudley what it meant.

Dudley said that he had heard that the Salem magistrates had asked Father to conduct examinations of the accused. Father's letter said something like, "I am not acquainted with affairs of this nature, and have found myself in service for which I am totally unfit. I beg that my ignorance be covered for. I do not know whether to make any indictments."

Dudley asked what I thought of the letter. He has hardly ever in his life wanted to know my opinion, and I believe it was to test me to see if I have any mind at all.

I said I was disappointed in Father's decision, since if Father were to do the examinations, then he would know that Polly's mother and aunt were innocent.

Dudley shook his head at me in his old way as though I were a simpleton. He said that Father is perplexed and knows not what to do. Father's letter does not take a position, and is foolish.

I said, "Father is not foolish!"

He said Father was not foolish but the letter was so. I felt strange to defend Father, when I have said I hate him. Dudley said that I do not understand. Then he said something that I truly do not understand, that Father is not so angry with me as he appears. I believe Father is even more angry with me than he appears, as he speaks little to me and is cold and far away.

Mother would not allow me out today save to feed the livestock and gather the eggs. It was perishing hot, yet I had to stay inside and do handwork. Mother's eyes were red and she looked grim. It may be the anniversary of the day that Annie died, as I remember last August Father told me that was why Mother was weeping. He said that the heat reminds her of her suffering then. Mother has told me it was a hard delivery and that she was sick for two months after.

I worry sometimes that I must marry and bring forth children. How can a woman bear the pain, and what if the child should die? When Molly brings forth her piglets each year, it seems nothing, yet so many women die with the child. Perhaps that is easier than watching them die alone. I am afraid to come to the birthing table. Even marriage to someone like Job would be fearsome.

I helped Ruth make the midday meal, and Father came home for it. He looked ill also, and he and Mother did not speak except for the passing of the flagon of pear juice up and down the board for all to drink from.

There was a knock on the door, and I thought it sounded like an omen of unhappiness. There was a time when there were no knocks upon the door, and now there are many, all unhappy.

It was Reverend Dane, and although we were not finished eating, Mother and I left the board to go to the kitchen. I could see that Mother was torn between listening herself and talking to me so that I would not hear. As Father and Reverend Dane spoke, she could only listen, as it was so strange.

Reverend Dane was not angry as two nights ago. Instead he began most quietly,

"You know, of course, they have taken Abigail."

I thought about when I had seen him and Goody Ffaulkner at the store, she in her beautiful pink shawl with the fringe.

Father said nothing for a minute and then,

"On this day when I am grieving for my own lost daughter I grieve for your daughter as well, and hope to God that she shall not be lost."

"Did you know that she is with child?"

I did not hear Father's reply but I imagine that he did not know, as I did not.

"Look at me, Dudley Bradstreet, and tell me that you have no fear. If it is my daughter today, it could be yours tomorrow."

I had never thought this, even for a minute, not even when I had my bad dream of the tiger, and I could not listen as the thought swept through me. I felt far away, as though all around me was unreal, and my white-faced mother, too frightened to send me away, was no more real than the knitting on my lap nor the dirty trenchers I could see upon the board from where I sat.

When I could attend, Father was saying, quiet still,

"... not then, at first. As you know, I thought Goody Carrier could well be a witch. When the Salem girls came to the Meeting House, the blonde one, Ann, made me think of Joan of Arc. She was so passionate, so piteous. I could see Satan and the Holy Spirit fighting for dominion in her visage. If she pointed to Goody Foster, it must be so. And the others since they were but relations of those two. And now there is Martha Sprague. She seems most truly possessed, I have no doubts of that, but I trust her pointings less, especially since they have become directed at your kin."

I was hurt that he did not say he mistrusted Martha's pointing to Polly's mother.

"Martha's friends, Rose and Sarah, are now also barking and fainting," the Reverend said, bitterly. "What does Martha say that my Abigail has done?"

"She has tormented and afflicted her, and something about a fall from a horse," Father said.

"It is I she despises, and my preaching which torments her," the Reverend said. He left soon after.

Fourteenth of August

This morning Reverend Dane preached to my father, I felt. I watched Father and he looked directly at the Reverend and the Reverend directly at him. In truth there was but a handful besides our family in the Meeting House. It was fearfully hot again today, and the sun burning through the glass windows upon my face was a torment.

Reverend Dane's theme was "a voice crying in the wilderness." It was about crying out and speaking for what one believes, regardless of the consequences. We cannot all be like Christ, willing to be crucified for our faith, but we must try ever to speak our belief. I felt the sermon spoke to me, as well. It is not wrong to speak my belief to Father even though he sees it as disrespect.

After the service I spoke to Hannah, who was wearing black, and was grieving for her aunts and cousins in the jail. Her face looked pale beneath her widow's peak, and I found myself thinking about why hair like hers should be called a widow's peak. There is in truth a sad look about it. She said that she felt that her grandfather spoke to her in the sermon, that she must be brave, and that coming to his service itself is a form of bravery like speaking out. She fears for herself and her family, since so many of her cousins have been taken.

Perhaps a good sermon is like that, in that each feels that it is spoken to them alone.

I have a fear as well, that Martha shall not rest till all who saw her at the Cochichewick Brook with the Witless One shall be arrested.

In the afternoon, all of Andover came, and Reverend Barnard preached again about the end of the world. He spoke of how four wells have dried up in the last week, and many are hauling water all the way from the Shawshin, and the Cochichewick Brook is already dry as a stone. All the crops are failing and we shall starve this winter. The air in the Meeting House was suffocating, and the sun still poured through the windows, though upon the other side. It was hard to take a breath. In the middle of the sermon the Hussy fainted away. After, I heard Eunice Frye say that it is because she binds her waist to make it seem smaller.

The heat within the House made the Reverend's theme strike stronger. Our garden looks so poorly, and Uncle John has not come to visit. He spends all his days hauling water from the river to pour upon the crops. The Reverend said the drought was a sign that we are in God's disfavor. If we, who try hard to please Him, are in His disfavor, then all the World must be in disfavor, the drought must be everywhere, and no help to come from London or beyond, only starvation and peril unlike any other. He said an army of Devils has broken in upon the place which is our center. We must root them out or perish.

I came home in a great perplexity of spirit, and thought throughout the rest of the day. As we fell asleep last night, I said to Dudley that I thought I understood a little. "It may be that the end of the world is at hand, and it may be that we must do all we can to catch the Witches who are at fault. Martha Sprague, however, is not truly bewitched but only playing a wicked game, so Father must be encouraged to stand up against her and her friends, though many people will believe Martha instead of him, and it puts our family into danger."

"Yes," Dudley replied, "though Reverend Dane would have it that the end of the world is not at hand, and that there may be other bewitched girls who play a wicked game."

I had not thought about that, that some of the Salem girls could be like Martha. Surely not the pale one named Ann.

Dudley said that he and Job were going to play truant from school on Friday to go to the execution. Goody Carrier is to be hung from Gallows Hill, along with four Witches from Salem. Dudley said he has heard that the previous hangings were a sight to behold, with folk from everywhere. He said that perhaps there will be a sign to mark if they are truly Witches.

I lay there in silence, still too warm to sleep. I would not go to a hanging for any amount of money or God's forgiveness of my sins, yet I could understand why Dudley and Job would go. If the accused are Witches, there must be some sign of God's disfavor, and if they are not, surely God would not allow the hanging.

Fifteenth of August

Today Sarah came, breathless as usual, to tell me that another was arrested. Twas joking Goodman Samuel Wardwell.

Sarah said, "He told James Bridges that James was in love with a fourteen year old girl, and it was true! How could he know?"

I realized I must never say that Ruth can tell fortunes.

"It is mostly Martha Sprague who has accused him, however," Sarah went on.

"He was there when Martha fell from her horse in front of Peters' store. Twas his fault, she said, and in addition he sticks pins into her and pinches her mercilessly." My heart sank to hear that Martha was accusing more folk. I wished I could speak to Sarah and Hannah about my fears about Martha. I know that Polly is not a Witch, and I know that I am not, but it matters not. Martha will act against us.

I answered the door this morning to the Reverend Dane's Joseph. Ruth usually answers the door in the morning, and Joseph looked disappointed to see me. He said he had been sent to see where Dudley was. When I said to come in to see if anyone knew, he smiled, and went straight to the back room to talk to Ruth.

When Mother came from outside where she had been gathering eggs, she saw Joseph and guessed instantly that Dudley had gone to the execution.

"That boy shall have a whipping," she said.

Dudley returned home at the evening meal looking like he had already been beaten.

Father said, "Are you happy with your bad behavior?"

Dudley said, "I am not. Whip me and be done with it, I care little."

Father said that instead for his punishment he must tell us what happened.

Sometimes I believe I received my curiosity from Father, the way Dudley received his small feet. They are smaller than my feet which is vexing. In this case, partly I wanted to know what had happened and partly I did not want to hear at all.

Dudley said, "Maggie as well?"

Father said, "If she is sent away, she shall press her ear to the staircase regardless."

I blushed, but I did not go away.

Dudley's head was bent, making it even harder to hear his voice, low, not like his usual sermonizing. He said that the two of them had gone with Job's father and grandfather to Salem, sitting on the back of the wagon, with the breeze from the cart's movement providing a bit of coolness from the sun. That was the only pleasant part of the day. Father said that Dudley was avoiding talking about the hanging.

Dudley pulled at his knuckles as he said that there was a huge crowd at Gallows Hill, waiting for the open carts to come from the jail. The crowd grew and grew, most people coming like Dudley and Job in farm carts, but some gentlemen and even ladies as well in carriages. After a while, Reverend Cotton Mather arrived on a large white horse. He stayed on his horse near the gallows at the top of the hill so all could see him.

Finally the carts from the prison rolled in. The road to the gallows is little traveled, and it is potted, so the carts bumped and lurched up the hill, almost spilling the prisoners out. In the first cart, there were the five to be hanged, and in the second, there were Richard and Andrew Carrier, who were brought to be forced to see their mother hung. The five to be hanged were standing, and at the start of the ride up the hill, Richard and Andrew were standing as well. When their cart hit a grievous rut, the two were thrown to the floor. They did not get up again, and lay huddled in the corner of their cart.

Dudley's voice grew even harder to hear. He said he had felt ashamed that he had come on his own to see what Richard and Andrew should be forced to see. From that point he did not want to be there, and wished he could leave, but could not, as the crowds were so heavy.

Goody Carrier was in the first cart. Dudley said she was still the same, screaming out to the crowd that she was innocent. I asked what she was wearing, and Dudley said something brown. Probably the same worn petticoat that ripped when the constables pulled her from her children, I thought. There were four men with her in the cart. Two of them Dudley did not know. Of the other two, one was John Willard, who had been a constable in Salem. Dudley told how Willard had arrested several Witches and then decided that those he was arresting were not Witches. He said he would arrest no more, and resigned. Then he was accused of Wizardry himself. He escaped and was caught, tried, and convicted, and now he was to be hung.

Father sighed and said, "I know John Willard, and his story. They took his goods, as well, and left nothing for the support of his family."

I asked, "Is he then a Witch?"

Father did not reply.

The other man that Dudley knew of was Reverend George Burroughs. Father and Mother knew him also. Dudley explained for me that Reverend Burroughs used to be the Salem minister, after a fight over his salary, he had been asked to leave. He became a minister in Maine, and back in May the Salem constables had gone to Maine to get him. They came into his house while he ate his midday meal and carried him away. They say he was the ringleader of the Witches, worse than any, and many had testified against him.

Reverend Burroughs was the first to be hung. As he climbed the ladder to the gallows, he asked to speak. He was a short and puny man, and Job's father said it was a part of his Devilry that he could do superhuman feats of strength, like carry huge barrels that larger men could not even lift. At first he could not be heard through the jeers and taunting of the crowd. Finally the crowd stilled.

Dudley said, "He spoke gently and with wisdom. He protested the innocence of all five of them, in the presence of God, whom they were soon to appear before. He wished that their blood might be the last innocent blood to be shed. He entreated Reverend Mather to pray with them."

Reverend Burroughs led the group of five in a prayer that God would discover what actual witchcrafts were among the people. They forgave their Accusers and the Judge and the Jury, and prayed that God should pardon these deceived men and women. They prayed earnestly for pardon for all sins they had committed in their lives. Then Reverend Burroughs recited the Lord's Prayer without hesitation or error.

I burst into Dudley's tale. "Such a thing is not possible. No witch can recite the Lord's Prayer."

Dudley nodded. "All about me people were crying out, 'Free him, he cannot be a Wizard.' I noted tears in the eyes of many in the crowd, especially the women, and even Job had wetness on his cheeks and was crying out to free him. I cried out myself. People began to push against the platform. Then from his high white horse, Reverend Mather spoke out, loud above the noise."

"He said that Burroughs was not an ordained minister, that a court had found him guilty, and that we must be a people which trusted in our laws. He said that the Devil has often been transformed into an Angel of light. People stopped shoving, though there were still some cries. The execution went on but I could not look, and as I pushed away through the crowd I heard the snap of his neck, and the sigh that went through the crowd."

Dudley said that he and Job had gone away and had not come back until the crowds began to move away, so they knew no more.

None of us had any taste for our meal that night. I could not stop thinking about Dudley's tale. As I tried to sleep that night, I kept seeing Reverend Burroughs on the ladder in the hot sun, and Goody Carrier in her worn brown petticoat, standing with the men in the cart, screaming "I am innocent" and Richard and Andrew weeping in the other cart behind. I could see Reverend Mather upon his huge white horse with his wig like two red animals upon his head. I could smell the manure from the farm carts and the odor of too many people in the crowd, and the odor of fear from the prisoners. I could hear the snap of the neck, like when Stacy kills the chickens.

God did not cast a clear sign, but if there was any, it was the Lord's Prayer. How horrid to think that they were not Witches, and how horrid to think that they were.

Mother let me go out today to buy a spool of brown thread to mend Father's hose. She must have known that I would go to Polly's on the way, but she did not ask and so I did not have to lie. When Tobey and I got to Polly's, it was quiet, with none in the yard and no children crying in the house. I knocked upon the door with the iron knocker like a lion's paw. I was amazed to see Job Tyler open it, with a large broom in his hand.

"Come in," he said, holding out his arm and the broom to welcome me, as though it were his house.

"Is Polly at home?" I asked.

"No," he said. "I came by to help out, but I found no one at home. She cannot be gone far, though—come in and wait for her."

I blushed. I wanted to be with Job, and I wanted to wait for Polly, but I could not go into an empty house with a young man, even if he himself saw nothing the matter with it. He might have said, "You are not a woman, only a child."

When I blushed, his face changed. He said, "Wait till I finish sweeping, and you can help me weed the garden till she comes."

"It is hard for Polly to take care of things all on her own," I said, watching a powerful amount of dirt, a dead mouse and many spiders and bugs come sweeping out the door.

"My uncle is of little help. I expect he is in the tavern now, as he has been since Aunt Polly was taken," he said.

"I expect so," I said.

We walked over to the garden, which was in a sorry state, filled with weeds and dried out from the lack of water. Even the weeds were dry and scaly, but they were stronger than the plants. Job used the hoe on the weeds near the beans, and I squatted by the parsley with a sharp iron stick from the forge as a digger. I chose the parsley because I like the herbs, and tend to them at home. They smelled sharp in the heat, especially the parsley. I was wearing my old gray petticoat, so dust did not show much, but I wrapped it around me to keep it off the ground. Regardless of dirt, I would have worn a prettier dress had I known I would meet Job.

Job asked for my family's health, and I said they were fine, and I asked for his father's health, and he said his father was fine. After a pause, Job said,

"Do you not wish to ask for the health of my step-mother? And how about Martha?"

I blushed again and said that I wished his step-mother well but I could not think kind thoughts of Martha. Actually I do not like the Hussy either, but I did not say that.

I realized too late that he had been teasing me. We did not speak again for a time.

It was fearsome hot out there with the sun beating down. The garden sits to the south, so there was no shade of any kind. It was hard even to see in the brightness. The ground was as hard as iron, making it almost impossible to pull the weeds. Tobey wanted to play and I had to keep telling him to sit as he ran into me. His hot fur and warm dog breath made me sweat even more.

I knew I could not stay long as Mother would note my absence. I wanted to impress Job that I was old and mature and worthy of his notice, and I could think of nothing whatever to say. Before I knew it, I blurted out,

"Dudley told us you cried when Reverend Burroughs was hanged."

His face turned red. He looked at me to see if I was mocking him. When he could see that I was blushing more than he was, he said,

"That was the last hanging I shall ever go to if I live to be as old as Goodman Foster."

"I do not even like to see the chickens killed," I said.

We said nothing else for a time, and just as I was thinking I must leave, he said,

"I fear for Polly."

"I do as well," I said. "I fear that Martha will not rest until all who know of her threats to say she was bewitched are in the jail."

"You are at no risk," he said. "Your father's name protects you. A Bradstreet is not a Witch. But Polly has no name. All the women in Andover who have been arrested have also had their children taken."

I had not realized that, and what it meant for Polly. I was even more afraid for her. I left then, as I could wait no longer.

Twenty second of August

I do not want to be a silly wench, but I find myself thinking over and again about my conversation with Job. It was the first time ever I have been alone with a young man, even though we were surrounded by the beans and the parsley and our hands were dirty with the weeds. I think ever after the smell of parsley shall remind me of Job and that afternoon.

I curse myself for a clumsy child. I wish I had found a way to speak in a more adult or interesting way. I still blush when I think that I spoke of his tears at the hanging.

I fear for Polly. I was surprised that Job fears as well, and it doubles my fear. I have thought and thought. I must talk to Polly, but it is likely I cannot see her until the Sabbath. Mother noted how long I was gone for the thread, and charged me with going to see Polly. I said, in truth, that I had not seen Polly, but she saw the lying intent within me. She told me she did not believe me and said I must stay in.

I care not what Mother thinks of me, which is wickedness indeed. I am only troubled that I cannot go out and about.

I spoke to Dudley last night as we were falling asleep. At least Dudley fell asleep, I was awake for hours as I tossed about in the heat. The straw sticking through the mattress was another torment to tickle and make me sweat.

I told Dudley I had spoken to Job, and that Job is worried about Polly. "Yes," he said, "I heard Father talking to Constable Ballard, and I heard Polly's name mentioned among others."

I gasped. I could see Polly's face before me, as she had looked when she came to tell me that her mother was taken, not merry any more, with the freckles now standing dark against the pale, and I could feel again her desperation as she clung to me that night. "Whatever shall I do, Dudley?"

"I know not," he said. "You could speak to Reverend Dane. He is the only one to help, I fear."

I wanted to ask if Job had said anything of me to Dudley, but I could not find a way, and I was ashamed to have such selfish thoughts at the time I should be worrying only about Polly.

Twenty fourth of August

The Sabbath has finally come, and I had two errands to fulfill, one to talk to the Reverend Dane, and one to talk to Polly. I could pay no mind to what the Reverend Dane spoke at service, so intent was I on what I would say to him after. I did note that he spoke with little heart, and that it was hard to hear his high pitched voice in spite of sitting so near.

It was easier than I had feared to speak to him, as none approached him after the service, and Mother was stopped by Hannah's mother with a question about charity for the Wardwell family, who have nothing now that Goodman Wardwell has been put in prison for a Witch. This allowed me to slip away and follow the Reverend back to his house. He looked surprised when Joseph let me in. He sat in his high backed chair with his feet upon a stool, the shoes most worn. He pointed to a chair for me to sit on, and asked how I fared, until I burst out that I must help Polly, who might be arrested and could he help me.

He shut his eyes and said, "If I could not help my own daughter and granddaughter, I know not how I could help your friend. I speak out each week that folk should see the error of their way and trust one other once again, yet no one hears me. Not even your father."

"You could not hide her?" I asked. It was bold, and I knew the answer, but I also knew if I were not bold, I would regret it later.

He shook his head. "She would be found, and then all should be arrested, she, and I, and the rest of my family."

I began to cry. I had no handkerchief. Mother tells me a lady carries a handkerchief at all times. I cried into my sleeve, staining it with dirt from my face. When I could stop, he took my chin in one hand, and his own handkerchief in the other and wiped my face.

"I am sorry," I said. "You were my last hope."

"There is always God," he said.

"You have prayed and prayed, I imagine," I said. "Why does He not help, then?"

"I know not," he said, and I left.

I felt alone before, yet even more so now.

Twenty fourth of August, later

I made it back in time for our midday meal, and then services again. After they were finished, I hurried out so that I could catch up with Polly as she left the Meeting House. Polly looks ill—as thin

91

as famine and most pale. The freckles sit like sores upon her skin. I walked her along, and as I pulled her ahead of the children she was minding, Mehitable began to cry. I told Polly I feared she would be arrested soon. She turned even paler, and said she thought so as well.

"You must run away," I said.

"Where could I run to?" she said.

I had no answer. I said I would come as well, and that I could steal Hector and some money and that we would manage for a time until it was safe to come back.

"I cannot," she said.

"Why not?"

"Who will watch the children?"

"Your father will have to stay home from the tavern," I said sharply.

She said nothing for a while, and then said slowly, "Not you nor any can help. I must leave it in God's hands."

Then suddenly I had another idea.

"Why do you not hide at Mossy Green? There is water there, and many blueberries nearby. I can bring you food every day. You must take a blanket so you can cover yourself from the mosquitoes at night, and a knife and whatever food you can find in a tight-fitting pot . . ."

I thought of the tight-fitting pot as I have heard the story of a settler who went West, and took food which he left in his pocket. In the night the bears came and ate him up.

"I do not have a tight-fitting pot, and if I take the knife there will be nothing to cut my father's dinner."

"Never mind. Just you go, tomorrow morning, and I will come with everything you need."

Polly looked at me so intently that I was reminded of how I might have looked to the Reverend Dane, asking for help when he had none to give. I will help her, I will.

"I shall meet you there tomorrow morning," I promised, and I ran home. When I think of Polly as she was before, my dear merry friend who would count it a great adventure to run away and live in the woods, I think my heart could break.

Twenty fourth of August, later still

It is black outside now, and I am writing in the dark in my bed so this will not be written well, but I need to plan what I shall bring to Polly. I have already taken two things from my chest and put them under my mattress, the grey blanket that I use on my bed in the fall and winter, and my brown shawl that I seldom wear. Mother will not miss these things if I give them to Polly, who will need them for the cold at night.

In the morning I shall sneak quietly down before first light and before Ruth has begun the breakfast. I shall take

a knife

the brown earthen pot from the kitchen, with the cover that fits tight

much samp

dried pease for porridge

carrots from the garden

a slab of bacon, though she will not be able to have a fire as the smoke could draw attention and she will have to eat the bacon raw

the piece of pie that was left over from last night's dinner.

I fell asleep the night of the 24th feeling comforted in my plan, though I did not sleep well because I knew I must get up before first light. I kept waking up when it was still pitch black and wondering what time it might be and whether I should get up then. Finally I fell asleep for a long time, and wakened with the first morning light coming in through the chinks in the siding.

I pulled myself quietly out of bed, took the blanket and jacket from underneath, picked up my shoes and a petticoat to put over my chemise, and slipped down the stairs, trying not to creak the boards. None in the family stirred, and I was pleased. Ruth was not in the kitchen yet, and I was pleased again.

I put on my shoes and my petticoat, and spread the blanket out upon the table, to wrap all within. When I lifted the brown pot from its shelf, I had misjudged its heaviness and it fell with a tremendous crash to the ground! Samp spilled all about in the midst of pieces of the pot. I heard the whole household start awake. Tobey began to bark and I had to act in an instant so I grabbed the piece of pie from last night's dinner and the blanket and ran out the door.

Tobey was behind the fence, and could not get out to join me, though he barked and barked. I ran as fast as ever I could south down the Boston Way, and I checked that there were none behind me before I turned east into the Newbury Way.

When I came to the hidden entrance for Secret Way into the forest for Mossy Green, there were still none behind me, and I pushed through the branches to the narrow way.

Polly was not there when I arrived and I sat there upon the bank. The moss was dried up, and brown and scratchy upon my arms. I sat looking at the dry stream bed with the cracks breaking it into pieces like a picture puzzle I once saw in Boston. I waited hours. The sun rose in the sky till it was overhead, at least as much as could be seen or felt through the overcast sky. It looked as though it might rain, though indeed it never did. It was hot and damp, with many mosquitoes, and I had to be alert to each small touch on my arm or neck so that I could slap at them. I was so hungry that I was sore tempted to eat a portion of the pie, though I knew I must save it for Polly, who would have no food, while I could return home. It was a sort I loved, a pie with pudding inside, flavored with maple syrup.

Where was she? What could have happened? Had she been arrested? What would my parents do to find me? My mind raced around and around these worries. Finally I was bored, even of my concerns. There was nothing to do but slap at mosquitoes. I wondered how I had ever come to think that going into the forest was an adventure. How would Polly stay here by herself? I then realized that in fact she would not be here by herself, as I could not return. Regardless of how I lied, Father and Mother would suspect I had gone to help Polly, and as soon as it was known she had disappeared they would be certain of it. They would beat me till I told where she was. Even if I could hold out, they would not allow me to leave the house, and I would not be able to bring more food to Polly each day as I had planned.

I felt like crying, but I swallowed the lump in my throat and got up and went toward the blueberry bushes. Since I was staying also, we would need even more food, and there was only what we could find in the forest. I took off my bonnet to gather the berries in.

I had picked it full, eating some as I went along to quiet my hunger, when I heard noises on the path. For the first time ever at Mossy Green I was not sure whether the noises were Polly or someone else, and my heart lifted when I saw Polly's white bonnet bobbing along through the trees at a fearful pace! It fell again when I saw that she was crying, and that she had brought nothing with her, no food or blankets, nothing. I ran to her and put my arms around her, trying to still her tears.

"Oh, Maggie, I was not going to come. Mehitable is sick and there is no one to care for her. But then I heard a carriage coming and I knew in my heart it came for me. I ran out of the house as I was, and ran till I got here."

"You did not see it," I said, "It could have been any carriage."

"It came for me," she insisted.

"You shall be safe here," I sat her down and fed her the pie. I watched wistfully as she gulped it down. The sweet pudding put a small smile on her face. When I said that I would stay with her she jumped up from the bank and hugged me. I could feel her body relax.

We picked more berries and ate them till we were heartily sick of berries. Polly found some wintergreen leaves, which have a fine flavor but are tough to chew and hard to swallow. We searched for anything we could eat, going in circles further and further from the banks of the creek. Then we walked along the creek bed, where we found a few purslane and dandelion leaves which were covered with dry mud. We would need to wash them; water was a necessity for drinking too. Even with all the berries I was thirsty already.

"There is probably water deeper in the creek bed," Polly said, reading my mind. Sharp rocks stuck out of the walls of the creek, and we pried loose a couple of them. On another day I would have pretended they were Indian axes. Today I could not play. We dug and dug, our hands and arms becoming covered first with dirt and then with mud. At last we had a small pool of dirty water, too muddy to wash our hands, let alone drink, but we thought the mud would settle out if we left it for a time.

"How will we ever find enough to eat?" I could see us starving here, even if we had water. Polly said we could go to Barker's farm further along the Newbury Way, and steal corn in the night. That idea sounded like the old Polly, and I felt better. We decided to wait till the next night to steal the corn, as there was a risk to it, and by then we would need food for a certainty.

When we could think of nothing more to do, we sat there on the dry mossy river bank under the oak tree talking through the rest of the afternoon. Polly said that Job would have come to care for Mehitable by then. He had promised her yesterday. Mehitable had a sharp fever and a vomiting. Polly talked much about Mehitable and how she worried about her, I think because it was an easier worry than about her mother or ourselves.

Polly talks of Job as she would of any cousin, and mocks him for the way he sometimes bites his nails. I do not want to keep a secret from her, but I feel shy about telling her what I feel about Job. I fear she would tease me, as to her he is so ordinary. I said that I thought it fine of him, a man, to come and care for Mehitable.

We also talked of what we should do if the constable came for us. We had not taken the Indian trail much further into the forest, as it narrows past the creek, but we decided we should follow it and perhaps there would be a place to hide.

As the sun approached the horizon, we picked the purslane and dandelions, and washed them in the water, which had indeed settled out by then. I do not care for dandelion greens as they are so bitter, but they tasted fine this day. We ate them, and drank some water, cupping our hands into the hole we had dug. Though I was still hungry I did not speak of it. Polly did not speak of hunger either.

The sun went down without a sunset, just a dull glow in the west, because the clouds were so heavy. As it began to darken, the animals came out, and we watched the rabbits play on the other bank of the creek. The deer would have found our water hole but we made noises and they ran away. There were only a few fireflies because of the drought. After the light was mostly gone, the mosquitoes became vicious.

There was nothing to do but try to go to sleep. I had never slept out of doors before, and knew no one who had done so. I thought of the man who had been eaten by the bear.

We went to the top of the bank where it flattened out, wrapped our petticoats around our legs so that the mosquitoes could not get through, and lay down. We put our heads upon the edge of the blanket, and pulled the top back down over us, so that our heads and arms were completely covered. As we were lying there, silent, each with our worries, I began to giggle.

Polly said, "What is it?"

I said, "At least if we have no food, we do not have to worry about bears."

It was not really funny, but we both giggled and giggled, and fell asleep.

It was hot with the blanket over our heads, and I kept waking up feeling stiff and uncomfortable. Polly must have been most tired with her work caring for Mehitable and the other children, and with our work during the afternoon providing for ourselves, as she was asleep each time I wakened. Sometimes she snored, though not so loud as Dudley does. Dudley tells me that I snore like the growl of a wild animal. I believe he is only trying to get back at me for my remarks about his snores, which make me think he will choke to death.

The ground was hard, even covered by the moss. I pulled the blanket off my head. It was so black that it looked no different than when I was covered by the blanket. There were no stars or moon, as the sky was still overcast with clouds, and I saw not even a lightning bug. I recalled my fears as a child, when I used to fear the Witches of the night. Two mosquitoes bit me instantly, and I tucked the blanket quickly back about my head.

I had thought the night was quiet, as the birds are still at night. There were sounds all about me. I recalled as a child how each creak of the house had seemed a Witch pushing in to find me, and each rustle of an animal in the wall had seemed a Witch about to jump upon me. Now there were creaks of trees, the wail of the mosquitoes, the wind loud in the trees, and many sounds I did not know, strange hoots and calls that could have been owls and other night birds and animals. Mostly there were rustling noises all about. I told myself it must be squirrels moving about. I could not calm myself. After a long time in which I felt more and more like the young child I used to be, I lifted the blanket again and peered about.

The rustling noises seemed louder and I could not see from where they came. I was bitten again, and I recovered myself with the blanket. At least the blackness was the blanket rather than who knows what.

I was afraid of Witches, but as the sounds grew louder, I began to be more afraid of bears. I remembered that bears love blueberries, and if bears came for berries and found they were mostly gone, they could be angry and come for us instead. The sounds seemed to grow louder and louder and nearer and nearer till I was convinced there was a bear and we must get up and run or rather move away slowly as one should not run from bears. My heart was beating ever so fast.

Finally I lifted the blanket off again and looked out. It was still black, but I was fearfully startled to see yellow eyes staring at me from three feet away, looking at me like a person would. I could see the eyes were too close to the ground to belong to a bear. In a minute the outline of a large raccoon appeared. The raccoon and I looked at each other for a long time. At first I thought he might be a Witch's Familiar, but then he seemed only curious. I understand curiosity, and I recalled that Indians believe they have kinship with certain animals. The raccoon was my friend, and I watched him till he moved away. I pulled the blanket over my head again and slept soundly for a time.

I woke with a sharp pain on my ankle, and then another. Ants! I wriggled my hand down and smished each thing I could feel on my ankle, and marveled that Polly still did not awake. At last I seemed to have killed them all, and I went to sleep again. This time I woke up too cold. I moved closer to Polly and finally fell asleep once more.

We woke up with the first light, bright even through the blanket, and got up feeling stiff from the night on the ground. Polly's arm was covered with bites where she had flung it out from under the blanket. My throat was so dry I could barely speak, and I hurried to our hole in the creek bed. It was gone, silted in during the night. There were tracks about the hole, looking like small hands, and I knew my raccoon had drunk there in the night. We would have to dig the hole out again, and wait for the mud to settle.

To take some of the thirst away, we went to the blueberry patch, and crammed all that we could find remaining, even those that were green, into our mouths. We found a small patch of huckleberries nearby and ate those too. I was still more thirsty and hungry than I could ever remember being. Polly did not speak of her feelings nor I of mine, but I knew she must feel the same. My belly cramped dreadfully from eating only blueberries and greens, but I felt better after I relieved myself behind the trees.

We began to dig again for water in the creek hole and talked about what we should do, follow the Indian trail further into the woods and look for caves, and go out at night to search for food from the Barker's farm. I wondered, though I spoke it not, how many more days we could stay there.

We were climbing up the bank, covered with mud, and I was talking of how Indians survive in the forest, eating acorns for one thing. I was picking one up from the bank to see how it tasted, when Polly grabbed me with her sadly bitten arm, and silenced me. We could both hear rustlings along the trail.

"Flee!" I cried.

We pulled our way up the rest of the bank and started running down the path deeper into the forest, abandoning the blanket. I went first, Polly close behind. Although the path was straight, it was narrow and covered with branches and roots. I tripped several times, righting myself with difficulty. Twigs whipped my face, and I heard Polly cry out when she ran too close behind and the branches

I was pushing forward snapped back at her like a trap hunters set for animals. Stickers caught in my petticoat. I heard it rip, and I could feel the sharp prickles through the cloth.

We had not gone far when I heard a familiar bark.

Tobey! My joy fast turned to dismay. Tobey could not help me. He would not be coming by himself, and he could run faster than me. They had brought my dog to track me down.

I had never run from Tobey before, except in play, but now I did with all my strength. It was not long before I felt his familiar breath upon my ankles. He ran ahead, as he does. I could not stop myself, tripped over him, and fell. Polly was right behind and fell over me.

Before we could right ourselves Constable Ballard and my father were upon us, puffing and sweaty. The Constable went for Polly, and Father went for me, pulling me back along the path till I felt my arm would leave its socket. Father spoke not, and his face was as red as the Constable's. When we got to the road, there were two carriages, one our familiar one with Hector at the front, and one the black fearsome one of the constable. My father pulled me to ours, and the constable pulled Polly to the black. We did not even have a chance to say good-bye. I wondered if that was to be my last sight of her in this world, just her dirty bare feet as she was thrust gasping into the carriage.

"Is she arrested, then?" I asked Father, and he nodded.

"And I am not to be?" I asked, and he said only, "No."

I burst into tears, in a tumult of feelings. I was sobbing for Polly, as I thought of her, hauled off to Salem in her dirty clothes, her body to be examined, people shouting questions at her. I was sobbing for me. Oh, it was good to see Father, to be out of the woods and to know that however I was punished I would soon have something to eat and drink. And I felt shame to have such feelings for myself, with Polly in such a state.

Tobey sat in back, panting and happy to see me. I thrust my arms about him and kissed his black nose. It was not his fault that he had chased me.

Father and I drove in silence. Father seemed not angry as I had expected, but sorrowful. He spoke only once, saying,

"I never thought my daughter should run from my home, to live like a savage and to run from me like a savage down the savage trail."

I felt sorrowful for Father and just a little ashamed I had hurt him. He drove badly, not paying any mind to Hector's pace. Hector went as slowly as he liked, and stopped at one point to eat grass by the road before Father spoke to him and brushed him with the whip.

I wanted to ask Father many things, but he was so silent I asked only one.

"Would Polly have been arrested yesterday if she had not run?"

He nodded. I was relieved, as one of my many feelings was worry that they had arrested her because she ran away, and that instead of helping her I had brought about her ruin. Polly was right about the black carriage coming for her.

When we turned into the driveway, I saw Mother waiting at the door. She ran to the carriage and to my amazement threw her arms about me and began to cry. Then she seized me by the shoulders and began to shake me hard until I thought my head would leave my body.

"Wicked, wicked girl," she said. And then she started to say, "To lose both my . . ." and she began to cry again and hug me and could not finish. It seemed she could not fix upon a feeling any better than I.

I was surprised that Father did not beat me. He spoke to Mother, not to me.

"Look at her. Filthy. No bonnet, skin red as an apple, clothes ruined, hands caked with mud, dirt on her face, covered with bites— wash her, feed her and send her to bed. We shall see about the stocks on the Sabbath."

I had already thought about the stocks, but I had not thought about what I must look like. Mother told me to take off my petticoat, and sent me out to the well in my chemise, with a bucket and a cloth.

"No more than a quarter full in the bucket, mind you," she said.

I primed the pump, and began to pull the handle, and as the water gushed out, I cupped my hands and drank and drank, and splashed my face. It tasted fine, and it felt wondrous on my skin, though it made the insect bites sting. After there was enough water in the bucket, I washed as much as I could reach with a cloth. Then I stepped into the bucket, first one foot, then the other, to wash my feet, turning the water black. I enjoyed feeling clean, though my shoes were so filthy and ragged that my feet turned dark again when I put them back on. I threw the bucket of dirty water on my herb garden.

Father spoke truth that I had ruined my clothes. My petticoat and chemise went to the rag pile. Mother sent me to find a clean chemise and a comb for my hair. She combed my hair herself, tutting at the snarls and pulling more than I liked. She fed me samp and it tasted better than almost anything I had ever eaten. I thought of Polly again, and hoped that she had something to eat, and a chance to wash. Then Mother sent me to bed, though it was not yet noon.

I had expected to be beaten, at least. I had expected to be put in the stocks on the Sabbath. What I did not expect was that when I moved the board in the wall and reached for you, my Book, you were gone!

I could do nothing but wait impatiently for Dudley to come home. He would know what had happened and would tell me, though if he had read my book he might not speak to me at all. I waited and waited, and then I fell asleep, so tired I only wakened with the sound of the outside door opening. I assumed it was Dudley, but it was Father.

"They have found a witch's tit upon her," Father said to Mother.

I knew in my heart they spoke of Polly, and I could not restrain myself. I ran down the stairs in my chemise and burst out,

"Where? Polly has none such upon her. We have bathed in the Shawshin and I have seen her body and she has no witch's tit."

My father looked stern.

"You know you are forbidden to swim at any time," he said. I thought he would tell me to go upstairs again, but I believe he was also curious. As I have said, we are alike in curiosity.

"It lies upon her belly in the center of her chest, where one would expect it," he said.

"She has nothing there. I know it. It must be but a mosquito bite. She is covered with mosquito bites. Did you not see them upon her arms?"

"I did not of course examine her, the women did that."

I had an image of Polly stretched out weeping upon a table and a group of stern women staring and pointing at and touching her naked body with its small breasts.

"Oh Father, whatever wickedness I have done, you must not think badly of Polly. It was my idea to hide in the woods. She has done nothing but follow my wicked lead."

"I know that."

"How do you know?" I was puzzled.

He did not answer me.

"Did Polly tell her examiners that? Tis not like her." I thought aloud.

"I have read your account of all your wickedness these past months," Father finally said.

I was ashamed of my wickedness revealed, but I was also angry.

"You promised no one should read my book," I said.

"I think that you should not accuse others of speaking false and breaking their word," he said. "When you had run away with no sign or notice, there was nothing else to do to find you. I would not have thought of that old Indian trail. I do not know it, and was glad of Tobey."

"I thought I had hidden my book well."

"So you had, but Ruth found it during her cleaning."

How could she tell my secret! Perhaps my face showed my feeling, as Father said,

"She worried about you also. Did you not know how we should fear for you? In the woods, with the Indians and wild beasts? Only Dudley said not to worry, that you would be able to care for yourself."

I was glad of Dudley's faith in me.

I said honestly, "I thought little about your fear, and more about my fear for Polly. I knew I should survive, but Polly may hang for a Witch."

I decided to push further. "Since you have read my book, you know that Martha Sprague is not bewitched, just a wicked girl who wants revenge on those who know her wickedness."

Father looked at me straight and said, "Men who know more than you must deal with these questions. Go back to bed."

"Might I have my book back?"

I expected to be beaten for insolence, but Father without a word took it from his pocket and handed it to me. I thought perhaps he wanted to know more of what wickedness I would do in the future. He again seemed to see my mind.

"We shall not read it again unless you run away again," he said.

Perhaps in spite of what he said, he felt he had done wrong to read it. When I went upstairs, I spent the rest of the day writing and writing, all that has happened up till now.

Tis troubling to think that Father and Mother have read my book. Tis terrible to have all my private thoughts so open. What I wrote about Job, for one. I cannot bear to think of them laughing at me, or telling someone. What if they spoke of it to Dudley, or worse, let him read the book?

And then I leafed through the pages and saw so many wicked things I have done, like letting the pig out, and lying about going to Polly, and sins in my thoughts, like not attending to sermons, and caring for material things, and then I found the place where I said I hated Father. I know not how to look at him.

Twenty seventh of August

Dudley came in late last night, after helping Uncle John harvest corn. Dudley said he had always wanted to stay all night in the woods. I was surprised, as I think of Dudley with his head in a book and not interested in anything but religion and telling on his sister. If he is Job's friend, he must have more spark in him than he shows to me. Dudley had many questions for me, such as had I seen any wild animals. I did not speak of my fear, but I made a story for him about being wakened in the night by loud noises, and then the yellow eyes. His own pale eyes grew wide in that way he has. He was disappointed that it was only a raccoon. He thought there might have been wolves and snakes, which I am glad I had not thought of.

He said much had happened while I was away. It seemed a long time to me, and I realize it was but one day. Five others were arrested, none of whom I know well. One is the daughter of Captain Osgood, who confessed that she became a witch after her mother died and she was overtaken with melancholy. How odd that Martha Carrier was taken for murdering Captain Osgood's wife, and now Captain Osgood's daughter should be taken herself.

Dudley said that since reading my book Father had gone to talk to Reverend Dane.

"Have you read my book?"

I tried to ask the question as though I cared not.

"Why should I care to read your silly book?" he replied, like the Dudley of old, which let me know that he had wanted to but not been allowed. I let out a large and thankful breath.

In the morning, Mother set me to chores at once. With tears in her eyes, Ruth embraced me so hard that my ribs ached. I thought how she was like Mother in some ways, though less strict and angry, and how Ruth would never shake me till my head threatened to come off. As I write this, I fear it shall not be private to me, and that I should not say such things. It makes me sorrowful. I think I must write what I feel regardless. If you read this, Mother, and it pains you, tis your own fault for breaking your word. You shall think me an ungrateful daughter. I am not totally ungrateful.

Ruth must have had thoughts like mine, because after Mother left on errands, she began to talk to me. I ground samp and Ruth chopped cabbage and neither of us looked at the other while she told me about her own lost girl. She loved a man and had a child in the West Indies but both had been separated from her, and she was sent North to us. I asked was she not married, and how could such a thing be. She sighed and said,

"This is how it is for Black folk."

I said I was grieved for her, and she nodded and turned her head away.

I charged Ruth with handing over my book, and she said she could not do otherwise.

"You should have seen the household. Your mother weeping, Dudley running all about to find you, Tobey barking, and I heard your father say, 'I have been too harsh.'"

I was amazed and gratified. I felt happy all through that they should have cared so, and happy with what my father said, though tis not good to take pleasure from others' pain. Again I hesitate to write down about my happiness lest others read it, and again I shall regardless.

Ruth and I cooked together like friends, making a stew of chicken and cabbage and the new corn Dudley had brought home, which is sweet and lovely, however small the ears are this year. We seasoned it with sage I picked from the herb garden. I felt so good to be there, and not to be out in the forest without food or water. To be sure, our vegetables are a disgrace, the well is almost dry so that we can no longer water the vegetables, and the chickens are laying less because the grain we put out for them is less, but I do not feel pain in my belly nor the fear that I shall starve.

After we had laid out the midday meal, the others came home from work and errands and school. I felt shy to see Father, knowing he had said he had been too harsh. He seemed harsh again, and looked little at me. I wanted to ask about Polly, and about Martha, but was not allowed to say anything. I said a silent prayer for Polly, that she would be set free and that she had enough to eat.

After eating, I was sent outside to feed the pig the shreds of cabbage from the preparation of the meal and the chicken bones we had left on the trenchers. I was told to stay outside. It took Molly but a moment to devour the food. Then I sat by the back door. Because it was so hot, the door was open, and I could hear most of what was said.

They were talking of whether to have me put in the stocks on the Sabbath, since as magistrate Father would have to decide my punishment. Mother said that it did not look good for the family to have me in the stocks. Father said that principles were principles, and that it did not look good for the family to set me to a lower standard than others. Mother asked how many knew of my wickedness, and Father said that soon all would know.

Dudley said, "Job Tyler says that it is partly his fault, as he told Maggie that Polly was at risk of arrest."

My spirits soared that Job would try to help me. Of course, he likely felt I was a helpless infant who would not have acted had he not planted an idea in my mind.

Father responded only, "Dudley, go back to school."

Dudley left through the front door, so I did not have a chance to thank him.

After Dudley left, there was quiet for a time, and then Mother said to Father,

"You remember your own stay in the stocks. Was it helpful for you?"

I blinked and sat up straighter. Had I heard right? Father in the stocks? Whatever for?

"You are bold to remind me," Father said crossly. "That was a long time ago, when I was a young man with rash notions."

"Shooting off your gun in the meeting house was rash indeed."

Father? Shooting off his gun?

"I was drunk, and John had a bad influence upon me."

"You sound like Maggie, casting blame about. Standing in the stocks does not seem to have helped you take responsibility for your misdeed."

"What is your point, woman?"

"I do not think that Maggie's rash unruly behavior will be changed by standing in the stocks. She will be the object of scorn, and it will harden her in her ideas. As you know from reading her book, she believes she has done the right thing. More important, I fear what could happen to her if others say she has helped a Witch. You think we are invulnerable, but I am not so certain."

Father sighed. "I want not to appear to be favoring my daughter. All will know that she has helped one who is accused of Witchcraft."

I was glad to hear my father refer to Polly as an accused Witch, not a Witch. Mother said, "It is one thing to know, and another to call attention to the fact."

109

Father said, "I have more important matters to attend at the moment. I must write a letter to the Salem magistrates, and the drafting is important."

I heard him leave, and I went back to the garden to weed till Mother should call me. I hoped that Father's letter to the Salem magistrates should free Polly, and bring wrath upon Martha Sprague's head. I was surprised at Mother's arguing with Father, as her habit is to be dutiful. I see that she fears for me, and for all of us.

I have thought several times about Job's defending me and what it might mean. I make too much of it in my thoughts, I am sure.

Twenty eight of August

Father took me aside after the evening meal and said he wanted to speak with me. He seemed stern, but not angry. I was excused from helping Ruth clear the board and Dudley was instructed to help instead. Father and I went outside to the garden where no one could hear, not even Mother, and as we faced the withered beans upon their poles he said,

"Maggie, I have been too harsh with you."

I knew from Ruth that he had said this, but the words themselves delivered to me were still hard to fathom. I blushed, I was so pleased.

He went on, "You have done some wickedness. There were sins that you recognize and that you must repent for, like lying to your mother, and letting the pig out, but running away itself was perhaps the largest sin, to worry your parents and challenge their authority in such a way."

I thought of saying that however wicked I was, I had never shot off a gun inside the meeting house, but I kept my mouth shut.

110

"Nevertheless, your heart was well-intentioned and you acted from love of your friend. Polly has confessed, I should tell you."

"Oh no!" I cried out. After a few moments I was not so surprised. Polly was so dispirited and worn down at the time she was arrested that she might have spoken anything.

"That does not mean she is guilty," I began and Father stopped me,

"I am writing a letter to the Salem magistrates about disregarding confessions. Some who are innocent may have confessed because the interrogation is so severe."

If he wrote a letter surely she and her mother and aunt would be released.

"You had some truths about Martha Sprague that I should have listened to. I shall not attach importance to Martha's evidence again."

"Thank you, father."

"The error in your ways is that you see all from the point of view of your friend, not the picture as a whole."

When I asked him if he would show me the picture as a whole, he began speaking at great length, much more than I could understand, about spectral evidence, about Reverend Cotton Mather who is a wise man but may be deluded into thinking that the end of the world is at hand, about other people who had been arrested whom we knew and who were not likely to be witches, about the suffering in the jails, about Grandfather and the difficulty of governing a colony when the authority came from over two thousand leagues away, and about politics. At the end I felt more a child than before. What I took from it was mainly that I must not think only of Polly and her mother and aunt, but of any who might have been accused unjustly. What if they were all unjustly accused? What if the real Witches had bewitched us so that we saw black for white and good for bad?

My mind whirled about. I could see I had been too narrow in my thinking. I had thought of the possibility that the five that Dudley went to see hanged were innocent, but what if the seven that were hanged before that were innocent, and what if all who were in jail were innocent, and all who were accused and still to be arrested were innocent?

"So why do you not do something?" I asked.

"I cannot be sure they are innocent," he said. "I am doing everything I can, standing by Francis Dane, talking to whomever I can, writing letters. I cannot turn the town around all alone."

The light had now failed, and the bugs began to bite, but before we went in I had one more bold question.

"Dudley said that you were not so angry at me as you seemed. He would not explain his meaning."

He said nothing for a time, and I feared he was angry at my question. Then he said,

"Dudley perhaps will be a good minister. Sometimes I think he has book learning only, and then at others I see he has some sense. You know that Reverend Dane preaches that only he who is without sin shall cast the first stone, and that no one is without sin. When one wants to throw stones, when one is angry at others, often it is because their sins cover up one's own.

"Do you recall the time when you were eight and Dudley was ten and he was so angry at you for stealing the molasses candy and eating it all yourself? He would have thrashed you if I had let him. I told him then that we become angry at those who are like us, especially when they do the very things we wanted to do but held ourselves back from. He wanted that candy like anything, and he was angry at you for doing the thing that he wanted to do."

I did not understand this well. Also I was not sure how it applied to Father, so I said,

"Did you want to let out the pig?"

Father snorted and said that he did not mean that. He said that perhaps he wished he could be as a child and shout, "That is not right!" as I did when Polly's mother was arrested, but the situation was too complex and he could not.

"Does that mean that Eunice Frye wishes to be a Witch? She is so angry at them."

"Hm," he said, "You know you must call her Goody Frye. I doubt she wishes to be a Witch. You must not think ill of others. Goody Frye is doubtless a good woman, yet I have thought that there are times that she has a wish to do harm to others as Witches do."

We went inside, my thoughts in a muddle, but ever so pleased that Father had spoken thus to me and that he was working to free the innocent. Surely Polly will be returned soon.

Twenty ninth of August

Mother sent me to pick blueberries this morning, so I took the route past Polly's house to Shoe Meadow, which has many berries. I had hoped I might see Job but there was no sign of him, and Polly's house was still and empty. I wondered if the children might have gone to Job's house, which would serve Martha right, as then she and her mother, the Hussy, would have to care for them.

I picked for a long time. The berries are mainly gone now, so I had to work hard to find them. I love the smell of the berry fields, which Father says smell of the decay in the bog beneath. Soon I would be picking apples, and perhaps Polly would be with me. I thought more about what Father had said, but in the main I felt happy, that Father loves me again, and that he is going to right the wrongs that have been done to those falsely accused.

The meadow was quiet, the birds too hot to sing. Then there was much noise crashing through the woods at the edge of the meadow, and I saw a bear! I began to sing "Onward Christian Soldiers" in a loud voice so it would see me, and backed out of the meadow toward the road, slowly, just the way that Father has taught us. I told Dudley later that it was the wrong song as I was not going onward but backward. I am glad that it was but a raccoon that night in the forest.

Then Ruth and I made pies. Today she let me help with the pastry for the first time. I have seen her cut the lard into the flour many times, and roll out the dough. This time I did it all myself. Though I got sticky hands, several times could not get the dough off the rolling pin, and the crust broke as I put it into the pan and had to be pieced together to stick in one piece, no one at dinner said, "What a foul pie." Dudley in fact commented that he loved blueberry pie.

It was such a good day that I often forgot to think about Polly. After the evening meal there was a knock at the door. How I have come to dread the knock at the door. This time it was only Reverend Dane.

Father rose to greet him, and motioned us to go into the kitchen. We did so and Dudley took up his book, and Mother her sewing and I my sampler, which is coming better than the last. I have finished, "If I of heaven may have my fill," and am on "world" in "Take thou the world and all thou will."

The three of us, even Mother, did not pretend to carry on conversation, and only listened to what they said.

"Brother," Father said, "I know what pain for you this day. I would I could have prevented it."

I had not heard Father call the Reverend "Brother" for some time.

Father was saying, "Another daughter and another granddaughter taken as well. I tried to see you today to warn you, but you were out."

His granddaughter? That could be Hannah, though he had many grandchildren. Would both my friends be taken?

The Reverend said, "That makes two daughters, and two granddaughters. I was to Salem to see the two, Abigail and young Lizzie, who are already baking in the prison."

Father asked for their health.

"The prison is so crowded I could barely to speak to them. There are no windows in this heat. I could scarce draw a breath, and such a stinking breath at that. And the vermin are everywhere."

I thought of Polly and her mother and her aunt, all crowded together in the heat and smells.

The Reverend was continuing, "Many are ill. Abigail's pregnancy pains her in the heat. She needs to lie down for the pain in her back, yet there is no room within that crowded room. She fears for her child. Lizzie has confessed, she has always been a foolish child, but I have counseled Abigail to hold firm."

Father said, "Tis Abigail's undoing that so many folk covet her position as a woman with money and property."

"Tis Abigail's undoing that she is my daughter."

Father changed the subject. "I have written today to the Salem court that confessions should not be taken as evidence, as the women are frightened out of their mind."

"I bless you. I hope that those taken today shall not confess. Young Gail especially. Though how can one take seriously anything that a child of ten says? And how can such a young child be a Witch in any event?"

I was relieved that it was Gail who was taken, not Hannah.

The Reverend went on, "Even young Lizzie who is most silly is not a Witch."

"She is not more silly than most wenches her age."

Both Father and the Reverend seemed to be trying to be nice to the other. They began talking of others in the community, and what they had said to each. I was reminded of the talks when Grandfather and Father come together, when I can not pay attention through boredom. Mother began to talk again, about the chores to be done tomorrow by Ruth, Stacy, and us, and how we should put up peaches. Dudley began to read his Latin in earnest. Then in the background I heard Martha Sprague's name mentioned several times, and I began to see that Father and the Reverend were talking of a plan. Most of the names they spoke of were the selectmen of the town, or others of good repute, and I heard Father say clearly,

"In the morning I shall go to see Reverend Barnard and say that I speak for all the right thinking, and that we wish not to rely on the testimony of Martha Sprague and her friends. Let us hope that there shall be no more arrests of your family."

They agreed it would be best if the Reverend Dane did not accompany Father the next day, and the Reverend left soon after.

Thirtieth of August

We worked all day on the peaches, which are small and shriveled, yet they begin to drop and the deer and mice will eat them if we do not. The tree is large for a peach tree, and Stacy climbed into it and picked. He filled the basket, lowered it down to me on a rope, and I took it in to Mother and Ruth. After we did three baskets, when he was mostly finished with the fourth, I called out to him that he had missed some fine fruit at the end of a branch. He moved out further and further, and suddenly the branch broke and he came crashing down through the other branches, with all the peaches flying. At first I feared he was dead because of how he lay. When he got up, all wounded dignity as though he were the King and had fallen from his throne, I laughed out loud. He had only sprained his wrist and scraped his knee. Mother was cross at all the bruised fruit.

We made pies, and this time I was not allowed to work the crust as there were several to make. We also cooked peaches for the winter, putting them in crocks and covering the tops with wax. With the bruised fruit we made preserves, though Mother is chary with the sugar as it is so dear and must come from England. Maple syrup does not work so well with preserves as sugar. Stacy put the last of the bruised fruit through our small press for juice.

Mother and Ruth and I cooked and cooked. The oven was hot for the pies and the steam rose for the preserving. After a time, we took off our petticoats and wore only our chemises, which were soon wet clean through. There were times I could not see because the sweat was running into my eyes so fast I could not wipe it away. The best times were when I was sent out to the well to fetch back water for us to drink.

Our hands were red from the boiling water, our faces were red from the heat and the kitchen smelt like heaven must. All the while I was sweating and measuring sugar and melting wax and chopping peaches, I was wondering in the back of my mind what was happening with Father and the Reverend Barnard, and hoping it would bring Polly home from prison. After what the Reverend Dane had said, I had a clearer picture of Polly in the prison, sitting crowded on a bench with others, no light or air, and the vermin. In that enclosed place the heat must be like Hell itself.

Father did not come home for a meal in the midday, as he knew we were preserving the fruit. There was no time for eating, only to sample the peaches as they were being cooked.

When the shadows grew long, we all collapsed, Father came home and we sat down and ate only leftover stew heated over and peach pie. The pie was delicious. Mother asked Father about his day, and Father said, "Fine," and asked Mother about her day. She told about the peaches and I told about Stacy falling from the tree. When Dudley laughed, Mother said to me, "Speak when you are spoke to."

Dudley then said, "Did you happen to speak to Reverend Barnard today?"

I marveled at his boldness.

Father said, "I did happen to. Why do you ask?"

Dudley lost his boldness here, and the meal continued in silence, with an occasional comment about the peaches or the weather or folk I am not interested in.

After the dinner Uncle John appeared. Mother asked after his health, saying he looked worn. He replied that the Shawshin was now too dried to haul water from, and that they were going to the Merrimack, which is so far that most of the water has jostled out of the barrels by the time they get back to the farm.

Dudley and I were sent outside. Of course I stayed near the door, and was not so surprised as I once would have been that Dudley stayed with me. Dudley wanted the place nearer to the open door, and we began to push each other as of old. We then stopped and worked out a way for each to hear though it meant sitting close to each other on the doorstep.

Father was saying, "I am disappointed. I told Barnard this morning that I spoke for many who had grave doubts. I told of Martha Sprague's carryings-on, and spoke of the cloud that must fall upon her testimony and that of her friends. I spoke as eloquently as I could, and yet I fear I moved him not. He said that he would think about it, and announce something at the service tomorrow. I fear he is too tied to Mather, and that we shall rue that connection. I note Barnard left soon after, and I would not be surprised had he gone to Boston to consult with Mather, though it is a long trip there and back before tomorrow."

Uncle John left soon after, and we were called back in. I know not what to make of what Father said. He is the magistrate. Why can he not simply say "We shall stop finding more Witches."

I found it hard to sleep again last night, and going through the alphabet for things of comfort did not help as my mind kept going off onto worries. What would Reverend Barnard say tomorrow, and why does he have so much power that Father should fear him? Would I have to stand in the stocks and what taunts or spitting should I have to endure? How does Polly manage in the prison? What would the trials be like for her and her mother and aunt, would they be convicted, and would they be hanged? I remembered to worry for all, not only Polly. How they must feel if they are all innocent and what would it be like to be convicted of a crime one had not committed? I thought again of Dudley's account of the hangings, and my stomach turned. Dudley was snoring loudly, there was snoring from below as well, and I thought I should never sleep. When Tobey who had not been put out came up the stairs, he crawled next to me, I put my arms about him and then went to sleep.

In the morning, the bell rang for the meeting, and a different group of people came to hear Reverend Dane. Some of his family members did not attend. They perhaps fear that they too shall be arrested. Three or four of the community came back, and I noted Father greeting them and talking with them. I think they must be among those Father has spoken with. The Reverend was especially eloquent today and took as his theme his favorite, "Let he who is without sin throw the first stone."

I expected him to announce that I should stand in the stocks, and when the end of the service came with the last amen and he had not, I breathed a huge sigh of relief. I heard Constable Ballard ask Father what he had decided and Father said there was too much serious wrong-doing in the community to worry about childish pranks. The Constable's face turned more red than usual, but he did not dispute Father. If Father has the power to decide about me, why does he not have the power to decide about Polly?

I talked to Hannah, whom I had not seen for an age, between the services. How good to have a friend, even though she is not Polly. We arranged to meet to sew together, and Mother said we could on Tuesday.

The Reverend Barnard spoke in the afternoon. He preached again the end of the world at hand. He painted it bloody, how we should perish of thirst, our tongues hanging black from our mouths and Devils all about in glee. He said we cannot rest until each Devil in our town has been captured and punished. It could be that a mistake or two may be made, but any who is unjustly executed shall have passed from this vale of misery to live in paradise forever.

I know that rewards will come in the next life for suffering in this one. Yet if Polly were in paradise she would miss the pleasure of the apple picking in a few weeks, the taste of the pumpkin pie in the autumn, the smell of the lily of the valley in the spring, and she would never marry and sit by the fire in winter with her children and play peek-a-boo until all of them laugh. Tears came to my eyes, as I do not know what heaven is like however wondrous it may be, but I know what this world is like and I do not want her or any to leave it before their true time.

At the end of the service, Reverend Barnard announced that there were several accused who were to be arrested in the week, family of those who had been already arrested and who were known to be involved. However, after that there would be no new arrests from accusations from people in this town.

Nothing was said directly about Martha, but I looked around and saw her turn a splotchy color, and others were looking at her also.

The Reverend continued. He said that instead, on the next Sabbath, we should have the girls from Salem to this town. We must all come to the service, and the Salem girls will find out who still in the community is truly a Witch. There was silence and then a buzzing.

I turned to look at Father, across the aisle, to see his reaction. He looked puzzled.

After the service, all could talk only of the coming of the Salem girls. I heard Sarah's father say to Father that it could be a true solution. Father said it was possible, that he hoped that might make an end to the matter. I asked Dudley later what he thought. He said that it would depend on which girls were sent, as some might be as wicked as Martha. I thought about that, and said I hoped that they send the girl Ann again. Dudley says her father is a Sergeant. I am sure she is not wicked.

I could see fear on many faces, as they looked around to think, would this one or that one be found to be a Witch, and what if they themselves were found to be a Witch? I have a touch of that fear myself.

First of September

I was happy to be sent to the store for sugar today, though the way is so short and it was fearfully hot and dry today, with the sun beating down. We are low on many things in the larder. Usually in the summer, we eat mainly vegetables from the garden, and this year since they are less, we rely more on last year's corn and wheat. Father buys these in bulk from Uncle John, but still we need more salt and sugar than usual for the corn and wheat. There are stores of rye which are being distributed to some in true need, though these have turned moldy.

As I went into Peters', there was a group of people hanging about outside in the shade. They were talking about whether it was hotter today than yesterday, the drought, the rising cost of everything because of the drought, how they would make ends meet, and who was at fault for it all. Then Eunice Frye came up. She said she had followed me all the way from where our houses adjoin. I wondered why she had not called out to walk with me. Probably she preferred to watch me to see that I did not dawdle or do something else that she could tell Mother. She said, proud as punch, "Well, I know who is at fault for the drought, and now they are going to pay the price. Today they have arrested seven." As the Reverend Barnard had said, they were mainly family of those already arrested. One was another grandchild of the Reverend Dane, Stephen Johnson. Thank God that Hannah was still spared. The one that caught at me the most was Becky Wardwell, the daughter of the fortune teller, who was taken with her mother and who is not yet one year old.

I wanted to cry out, "She cannot be a Witch, she is one of God's innocents."

I had a sudden fear for Polly's little brothers and sisters, Samuel and Elizabeth and baby Mehitable.

Goody Frye did not choose to walk back home with me either, though I enquired politely whether she would like to. She said she must talk to Goodman Peters about when more salt is coming in from England. I thought all the way home of all who have been arrested, making a list in my mind. Now I shall write it down.

Polly
> her mother
> her aunt

Martha Carrier, who was hanged
> her son Richard
> her son Andrew
> her son Thomas
> her daughter Sarah, who is seven

old Ann Foster
> her daughter Polly
> her granddaughter Polly, Jr.

Relatives of Reverend Dane
> his daughter Abigail Ffaulkner
> Abigail's daughter in law, Elizabeth Ffaulkner
> his daughter Elizabeth Johnson
> his granddaughter Lizzie Johnson

his granddaughter Abigail Johnson
his grandson Stephen Johnson
Samuel Wardell the fortune teller
his wife Sarah
his daughter Rebecca, less than a year old
his daughter Mercy
his step-daughter Sarah
Captain Osgood's daughter

Some others I hardly know—William Barker and his son and daughter, Susannah Post, Sarah Hawkes, Polly Parker, Edward Farrington, and a girl named Sarah. That makes thirty-one. I have decided that cannot be, so many Witches, and that many of them must be innocent. Those who are related to Reverend Dane, for instance, and Samuel Wardwell and his family, perhaps, as Martha is the main person who accused him, and what if all of them are innocent?

Third of September

Today, Hannah and I sewed, she on a quilt she is making in overstitch, and I on my sampler. By the end of the afternoon, I was three quarters through. Hannah says the colors are beautiful, and she is too kind to comment on my stitching. Even Mother said this sampler is much better than the last.

It was a long time since Hannah and I had talked together all afternoon. I have been so worried about Polly I have had little time for Hannah and Sarah. We talked of young men and I found myself confessing that I like Job Tyler, which I could never say to Polly because he is her cousin. Hannah promised not to tell, and told me she thinks that Stephen Farnum is well-favored.

We talked of course of Witches. It is a relief that there shall be no more arrests until the Sabbath, and then we shall be done. Hannah was afraid of what shall happen.

123

I said, "If the girls from Salem are honest, then you have no worries, as I know you are no Witch.

She said that she must fear because of her grandfather, and how all his family is accused. She dropped her voice, and said that she knows that many of the accusations must be false, as none in her family is a Witch, and it is clear that her grandfather is attacked through them. I granted her that, and praised her intellect, and said it had taken me longer to realize that so many must be innocent. I told her about Martha Sprague and the day at the cress and swore her to secrecy, although by now many must know. She gasped, and said she had never trusted Martha. She asked me then for details about how Martha had behaved to Thomas, and we began to talk of young men again.

I hope I am right, and that Hannah has nothing to fear on the Sabbath. I said to her that her aunt Elizabeth had come under suspicion because she was seen as a loose woman, and that her aunt Abigail had come under suspicion because she inherited her husband's money, and people were envious. The others who had been accused were their children. I think that her own parents will not be attacked, as they are ordinary folk. After all my arguments, I finished with,

"And how should the Salem girls know that you or your parents are the Reverend Dane's relation?"

"What if someone tells them?" she asked.

I felt a piece of her fear. It depends so much on whether the Salem girls are honest. As we parted, I suggested that to be sure perhaps she should not come on the Sabbath. She said that she had thought of that herself but was afraid her absence would occasion more comment and bring suspicion upon her.

"Surely you could have a megrim," I said, and she said she would think about it.

I am more worried than ever about whether what happens on the Sabbath will be fair and honest. I worry especially about Polly's brother and sisters. They are staying at the Tylers as I thought, and I asked Dudley this morning before he went off whether he thought the children might stay at home on the Sabbath. He gave me a different kind of look, and said Job had already spoken with him about that.

"Job would like to keep them at home, but can think of no way to do so. He would have to stay with them, and it would excite comment if he, a man, should stay away from the service to care for children. His step-mother and Martha have little love for the children, and would not stay home with them."

I felt I should have offered to help earlier with the children. How hard for them first to be separated from their mother, and then from Polly, and then taken to a place where they are not loved.

After Dudley left, I left Ruth to make the noonday meal and walked to the Tyler's, past the Witless One who was roaming by the dried up creek. I thought how much trouble had started from that day we had gone to pick the cress less than four months past.

There were children everywhere about the yard as I entered. Mehitable ran to me with her arms outstretched.

"Maggie, Maggie," she cried and almost knocked me over with the force of her brown small arms about my knees. I lifted her and kissed her dirty face. However dirty she may be, she always has the sweet smell of a child.

"She is such a filthy child," said a voice I recognized as Martha's, and her elegant form appeared from behind a tree.

"Perhaps if you took better care of her she would be cleaner," I said.

"I have plenty to clean of my own brothers and sisters without these extra brats," she said. She did not look so beautiful today, but had an ugly pout.

In that moment, I formed a plan.

"I shall have to ask my mother, but would you like me to take them for a few hours each day? Perhaps after the noon meal."

She said, "I should rather you could take them all the time."

"I shall start tomorrow," I said. "May we stay at their home? Goodman Bridges has gone to his brother's, I hear, and the children would rather be at home."

She shrugged. "It matters not to me."

I spoke briefly to the Hussy, and left, without seeing Job. He was probably helping in the fields. As I walked home, I thought about Martha's pout and how many children she must care for. I did not feel sorry for her because of the havoc she has wreaked, yet if she had not done such I could find it in my heart to feel some sympathy.

Fifth of September

Mother agreed I might watch the children each day as long as I did my other chores. She said,

"Perhaps you are finally becoming responsible." I did not dispute her.

Today I picked up Mehitable and Steven and Elizabeth. I did not see Job at any point. I spent the afternoon with the children at their old home. They were sad to see it empty. At least they had their familiar places, and they found old play things, like pieces of metal left from the forge to use as guns and bows and arrows. Steven and Elizabeth spent the afternoon playing a game of hunting Indians, taking turns being the Indian and the hunter. Steven tried to win even when he was the Indian, but Elizabeth did not allow it.

I think they will not suffer so much from the loss of their parents, as they are of an age and enjoy each other. Perhaps Dudley and I missed something in our childhood. It is Mehitable with her light brown curls all tight upon her head and her arms twisted tight around my leg that I worry for, as she is so young and can say nothing but,

"When will Mommy be home? When will Polly be home?"

I know not how to answer her but only pick her up and hold her sweet body to my own until the tightness leaves her, and she sinks into me.

Before I picked them up, I walked to Hannah's house and told her that tomorrow on the Sabbath she must come to the Bridges' house directly after the morning service and watch the children. We told her mother that the children needed care, and Mehitable especially needed attention as she tended to sickness. I believe her mother saw through our words to our intention, but fell in with the plan because she fears for her daughter.

Sixth of September

It seems a strange period of calm. I see few on my walks—today there were none gathered in front of Peters' store.

Two days ago at dinner Mother talked again of her wish to expand the back of the house. This time Father said we should do it, but not until next spring.

Uncle John came last night after dinner. He and Father talked late into the night, about crops and politics, not altogether about Witches.

Last night as we were falling asleep I said to Dudley,

"There is something I do not fathom."

He responded in his old style that there is much I do not fathom.

Ignoring him, I asked him to explain to me exactly what a magistrate is, and why Father cannot say, "There will be no more arrests in Andover for witchcraft."

Dudley sighed and said, "I shall refrain from calling you a ninny, but tis hard. You at least recall that you are a Puritan, and you may recall that Grandmother and Grandfather came from England as part of the group to found a Godly community, the City on the Hill, which would follow God's laws."

"Yes, I recollect that," I snapped.

"In England, Father would have more power. I am sure you recall the importance of Henry VIII."

Here he began a long discourse onto Henry VIII, his six wives, the execution of Anne Boleyn, and the separation of Church and State. From my mattress I could see across to his, and watch his arms creating faint shadows on the wall, as there were still candles lit below. I have caught Dudley practicing preaching, when he thinks none are at hand, and his arms move about in a particular way, just as they were last night. I am sure his eyebrows were also high on his forehead like an owl.

Of course I had heard of Henry VIII, but I knew little of his wives and how he had separated the State from the Church. Finally Dudley returned to the question I had asked.

"In Massachusetts, the power of the State lies beneath the power of the Church. The ministers are the authority, and with the elders of the Church make decisions about how the Community shall operate."

Here he began another long discourse about how many members of the community are not Puritans, and they cannot be members of the Church though they must obey its laws. And then more on the process of choosing members to be elders. His arms began to move again.

I was bored and vexed with him, as this was not what I had asked him.

Then he began on the Board of Selectmen and government within the town which Father must work with. He talked about the governing of the Colony, and how though Father is the Andover representative to the General Court which makes decisions, he is only one member. Then he went on to Father's loss of influence now that Grandfather is no longer Governor. And then on to Governor Phipps, and how he must do what he is told from England. If he wanted to stop the trials, even he would need to write to England, and wait months for the reply to come. Finally he concluded, "The Magistrate is important, but he cannot make decisions by himself. Were Father to say, 'There will be no more arrests for witchcraft,' the arrests would go forward and he would simply be arrested himself, like Constable Willard who was hanged the day in Salem that I went to watch."

I listened all through, more and more wrathful. I began,

"Why can you not answer a simple question with a simple answer? I am not a ninny yet I do not know about Henry VIII and the rest of it. Why do you go off spouting about something that ordinary people know nothing and care less about? Who gives a farthing about a woman who had her head chopped off more than a hundred years ago? I do not lord it over others with my knowledge. I have not spent my life poring over books, as you do, but I have learned useful things, like cooking, so that while you study I can work to prepare your meals and to mend your clothes."

I went on in this vein for a time and then I stopped. Dudley said nothing, for a change. I thought of what I had talked about with Father and asked myself if I was in truth this angry with Dudley. Is it possible that I wished to be like Dudley? Would I like to know about Henry VIII? Perhaps, I realized, with a pang. Not Henry VIII, but I wished to know about the woman who had her head chopped off and changed the life of the British forever. Had she been a girl like me who cooked and cleaned and played with dolls and had a dog, and did she love Henry, or did she marry because she had to, and what did she think when she walked out upon the place where her head was to be cut off? Did she think, "If only I had been a better wife?" or "Why did my parents force me to marry that detestable man?"

or "May God deliver me, even now!" or only, "Oh, oh, how blue the sky is and how green the trees!" I thought of Polly, if she is hanged.

"I am sorry," I muttered. "'Tis not your fault you are a boy and can go to school."

I had not realized till that moment how I envied him.

Dudley accepted my apology more gracefully than I would have thought, and offered me his history book to read. I doubt it has the knowledge I would like.

I was in fact a ninny. Why had I not seen Father for what he is? People did say he was the most important man in town, but I saw now that he was not more powerful than Reverend Barnard, and that Cotton Mather was more powerful than the Governor. I cannot find the word to describe my feelings. Disappointment is not strong enough. I felt with a wrench that I might never see Polly again and that she might be hanged. But it was more than that. It was as though the chair I had been sitting upon all my life had its leg break, and I was sent sprawling.

Seventh of September, 1692

A great many things happened on this day, and I shall write them as they happened.

When I woke it was raining, for the first time in a month, and it seemed an omen for good. In old times I would think rain an omen for bad, since I cannot go out in it. Because of the drought it seemed a blessing, little drops of life falling upon us.

It was the Sabbath, and tomorrow Dudley would go to take his examinations at Harvard, so that he woke early, waking me as well, and wandered about the house not knowing what to do with himself.

There were again a few new persons at the sermon of Reverend Dane, including Captain Osgood and his brother John, whom I had not seen at that service in many weeks. The Captain had much to say to Father but his voice is so soft I could not hear. The Reverend Dane preached about forgiveness and Mary Magdalene. I think Mary Magdalene would have been an interesting friend.

After the service, I did not tell Mother where I was going, for fear she should forbid me. I hurried to Tylers' who of course had not come to the morning service. My bonnet dripping, and my chemise clinging to my shoulders, I knocked at the door. All innocence, I asked for the children. The Hussy frowned at me,

"I did not mean that you should take the children on the Sabbath. The Reverend Barnard has asked that all be there today."

"I take them each day," I said. "I have walked a good distance through the rain to pick them up."

I added, "My father shall be annoyed should I return without them."

As I was speaking this, Job's blue eyes appeared over the Hussy's shoulder, looking at me intensely. I looked into his eyes, and dropped mine after an instant, so that the Hussy would not note our communication, which felt to me as though we were shouting. He continued to look at me throughout.

"Let them go, ma'am," Job said to her. "They need some time at their own home, with familiar things and with Maggie. It will not hurt them to miss one service. And it is a time you shall not have to tend to them, as well."

She let them go. I did not mention that it would be Hannah rather than I who would care for them.

Job's eyes held mine for that one instant only, and no words passed between us, yet I felt that all manner of exchange took place. I knew Job saw me not as a child. I did not care about my dripping hair and bonnet, as I knew that for that instant he saw me as beautiful, and I felt beautiful, though I know I am not. As I walked with the children back to their house, I sang Greensleaves, which is my favorite song, and I cared not whether Eunice Frye or any might hear or what they might think.

It stopped raining, so the children did not get wet. The sky stayed gray and there was not enough rain to do good. Hannah was at the Bridges' house to receive the children, and I left them with her.

I hurried back home, to find the midday meal finished, and Father and Dudley already gone to the Meeting House. Mother had waited for me. She began by scolding me most grievously for missing the meal, which I have never done before without telling her. I think she feared I had run away again. I explained to her what I had done, and she looked at me strangely, as though I were some changeling. She stopped scolding, said I was wrong not to tell her what I had done, and then,

"You are a clumsy girl, but sometimes you are clever. Cleverness can be good or bad, I know not which for you."

She asked me to fetch papers that Father had been working on, to bring to the Meeting House, and not to read them. There were many copies, with names just to fill in, and all said the same. They left blank places for names and as I recollect they said

_____ *being charged*
for that the said _____ *in or about the month of*
July last in the year 1692 in the Town of Andover in the County of
Essex beforesaid wickedly maliciously & feloniously a Covenant
with the Devil did make and signed a paper to the Devil and was
Baptized by the Devil. By which wicked Diabolical Covenant
with the Devil made by the said _____ *, she is*
become a detestable Witch contrary to the peace of our Lord &
Lady the King & Queen, William and Mary, their Crown and
dignity and the laws in that case made and provided.

My good feelings of the morning were gone instantly. I saw what
would be happening all too clearly. I was glad I had eaten nothing,
as I felt sick to my stomach.

The gong rang for services, and Mother and I walked together to
the Meeting House. The gray cool day no longer seemed a blessing
but an omen of ill. As we approached, she said very quietly,

"I fear what shall come today."

Crossing the threshold of the meeting house felt like entering
home when I know I shall be punished.

As we entered by the back, I was surprised to see Reverend Dane
standing there alone, while all others sat. Neither of the ministers had
come to the other's service for many weeks. He looked older than I
had ever seen, with his long gray hair grown thin and wispy. I went
to speak to him, but he shook his head no. He touched my hand, and
said, his thin voice sounding almost like a woman's,

"All our prayers are needed."

We passed down the aisle, past the Tylers. Martha and the Hussy
seemed not to note me, but Job looked up and was startled. I could
see that he was sorry I was there, and his fear for me first made me
happy, and then it added to my own fear. I had been thinking so

much about Hannah and the children, I had given little thought to myself. I know I am not a Witch, and I had felt Father's name would protect our family. We passed Eunice Frye, in black as always, and the Peters, and the Osgoods and Hannah's mother and father, and the Abbots, and all the families that I have known my whole life, and all the faces looked drawn. Father and Dudley were already seated, and Mother handed Father his papers across the aisle before we took our places. A few others came in after.

The Reverend Barnard spoke out loudly and firmly. He called upon God to be present and to help us in our work and to be with us in each step of the proceedings. He said that we should now, with God's help and the help of the poor afflicted girls from Salem, root out the evil that had lain among us for too long.

At that moment, our eyes strayed from the Reverend to the side door, as we could hear a carriage rolling up. When the door opened, a draft of cold damp air swept through and I felt Mother shiver.

Constable Ballard entered, with the same girls as before, the dark and the pale. The dark girl, whom they called Mary, looked heavier than she had in May, while Ann looked even paler and thinner than she had before. I was relieved to see that it was Ann who had come. She would not lie.

The girls looked haunted. Reverend Barnard called upon Father and asked him to sit at a desk which had been brought into the front, off to the right of the pulpit. Father carried with him his pile of papers.

Ann's eyes rolled back into her head. She shrieked,

"There is evil in this room," and then, over and over, "I am afflicted."

The hair on the back of my arm rose. Her voice sounded harsh as a crow's, but higher pitched.

Reverend Barnard commanded us to stand, as he brought forth a large quantity of handkerchiefs. He began to go up the aisle handing handkerchiefs to some. I knew not what the handkerchiefs were for, but I knew they did not bode well.

When he passed without handing one to me, or Mother, or Dudley on the other side, I began to breathe again. I had not realized I had stopped breathing. I turned and watched the Reverend go up the aisle, whether or not it was rude to stare. Everyone was staring. He gave handkerchiefs to many, perhaps more than half of the women. Hannah's mother received one, Eunice Fry received one. A number of children were given handkerchiefs, and I was relieved that I had kept away Polly's sisters and brother, as well as Hannah. I thought at one point the Reverend might ask for them, as he looked about him as though searching for some missing folk.

To my surprise, he gave no handkerchief to Martha or her friends or the Hussy. He gave none to Job. Job's eyes met mine again after the Reverend had passed, and we spoke without words our relief for the other.

He came at last to the Reverend Dane standing alone at the back of the Meeting House. I thought he might hand him a handkerchief. Some exchange took place between them, and at length Reverend Barnard backed away.

Reverend Barnard commanded all who had received a handkerchief to come forward and to stand facing the congregation. He told them to tie the handkerchief about their eyes so they could see nothing. I kept my watch upon those I knew best, Hannah's mother, and Eunice Frye. They were so pale. I thought about how Eunice Frye had spoken so often of Witches and their evil, and there she was now with a handkerchief upon her eyes. There were many there facing us, perhaps thirty.

The women looked as pale as Ann, who had begun to kick upon the floor as she had the time before. Mary, the dark one, was in a fit. She stood, but her body twitched, and flailed about. It was almost as though she danced. Martha's dance for the Witless One had been slow and smooth, and this one was fast and jerky, but there was something the same in both of them in the display of the body.

"Who afflicts you?" asked the Reverend.

Ann shrieked again, "Stop them, stop them, stop them, before I perish."

Her anguish seemed unbearable. She looked like she was dying.

"Touch her!" the Reverend commanded to Hannah's mother. I gasped that Hannah's mother should be chosen first. She staggered forward. I could feel her fear, the weakness in her knees. With the blindfold she could not see her way, and she almost trod upon Ann. When she reached down, she put her hand several places before she touched her upon the side of her head. Ann took a deep breath and relaxed as though she had gone to sleep.

It was uncanny how the stopping of her screeching made me first relax, and then when I remembered what it meant, and that Hannah's mother should be taken, the fear in me rose more than it had been before. I grabbed Mother's hand, which I have not done since a small child. Mother's hand pressed mine back. She was frightened too. It was all I could do not to stand and scream,

"Goody Dane is no Witch, she shall not go!"

Father began writing, and the Constable came and took Hannah's mother to a back bench where she began to sob.

I thought of Hannah, how she would feel, whether she would have wished to be here to know all of what had happened, even if it meant being taken with her mother.

Then I thought not just for Hannah and her mother and her father, but for what it meant that the Reverend Dane's daughter-in-law should be chosen first, and I felt not only fear and sorrow but anger. I looked back to see Reverend Dane's staring eyes, and thought that his face looked like a skeleton.

Ann was kicking and shrieking again, and I felt betrayed. How could she look so stricken and not be honest?

Others came, whom I knew but did not feel so deeply about. The Salem girls screeched and writhed and called like birds and dogs and cats and owls, until they were touched, when they went limp and quiet. Father was busy writing and writing, as more and more women were brought forward. His face looked blank and angry.

I knew that the girls were play-acting, that they were as bad as Martha, and yet in spite of that they struck me with fear. Ann screamed that she had lost her sight. She stared around as blindly as the women behind her in their blindfolds. She began to scream more hoarsely than before that her throat closed up upon her and she could not breathe. I was frightened to my bones. I could not help it. I had to pass water, I was so frightened, and it was hard to sit still. It was also fearsome to see the looks upon the faces of the accused as they were forced to touch and as they were pulled away.

Goody Osgood was brought forward, and I wondered if it was a punishment upon the family for returning to the Reverend Dane's services. The girl Mary stopped her whining at her touch. Father was slow to pick up his pen to write her paper.

Eunice Frye was called forward. She was as pale as birch bark and she swayed so that Reverend Barnard had to support her. If it had to be anyone, I would rather it was her, but regardless my heart went out to her. Ann stopped her gasping and twitches at the first touch from Goody Frye. Father wrote again. He was now done with the papers he had prepared, and had to write the whole thing out.

Job's aunt, Goody Tyler, was called, and the girls stopped writhing at her touch. I looked back at Job as she was hauled away to the back benches, and his face was tight with wrath. Now three of his aunts had been taken.

Then there were his cousins, the children of Goody Tyler. The twins are but eleven. They clung to each other piteously though they did not understand well what was happening. Joanna peed upon the floor, she was so frightened. The smell was strong. I could hardly control my own need, but I knew I could not leave.

Then there were two more children of Goody Ffaulkner. As they were pulled away crying I looked back at Reverend Dane. I thought he would go to comfort these grandchildren but Constable Ballard restrained him with a gesture. Father still wrote. I thought he looked more angry than I had ever seen, and very cold.

The noise of the crying and wailing of those taken was now louder than the noise of the Salem girls, and Reverend Barnard commanded that all those arrested be brought outside. We could still hear them, but the wails of the Salem girls were the louder noise in our ears, and the smell was less.

There were others. Captain Osgood's manservant was taken. Father was writing slower than before. I kept looking at the Eye of God upon the pulpit, and wondering how God could abide this.

There were still many more in front with handkerchiefs over their eyes. Till now, the girls had found all who had been brought forward to be witches. All who had been asked to touch the girls had been arrested.

Joseph, Reverend Dane's servant, was called. I heard a sound in back, and I turned about to see Ruth covering her mouth with her hand, and her eyes wide with fear. Joseph moaned, as he was guided forward to touch Ann. She sighed like she had just recovered from the worst illness one could ever have.

Reverend Barnard nodded to the Constable to take Joseph away. Reverend Barnard nodded to Father, who began to write. He seemed to hit a snag in the paper, as he stopped, and dipped the quill again into the inkwell. He picked it up again. Then, as Reverend Barnard was looking at the group of blindfolded folk remaining, deciding whom to pick next, Father flung his pen down upon the table. A large gob of ink flew from the quill in an arc like that an arrow makes from the bow, and landed upon the Reverend Barnard's hand.

"Fie upon this travesty of justice!" Father shouted louder than I have ever heard him. "You have called upon God, but He is not in this chamber! I shall write no more."

There was silence. Even the Salem girls were quiet, though they had begun their moans again after Joseph was taken. Then from the back Francis Dane called,

"You have spoken true, Dudley Bradstreet. God bless you."

Seventh of September, written later

As we left, I was reminded of the time Father had shot off his gun in the Meeting House, and I wondered if it had made so loud an impact. People had begun to mutter and look at us behind their hands. Father strode out, and Mother and Dudley and I came quickly behind with Ruth and Stacy behind. People were now beginning to get up and talk to each other. Without a magistrate, the meeting was over.

Once out of the building, Dudley and I ran ahead,

"I shall hitch up the carriage," Dudley said.

We knew without words that we must flee.

I went straight for the privy. When I had relieved myself, I looked back to the Meeting House and saw that folk had begun to leave. The Constable had begun pushing people into the large carriage, Joseph among them. Several trips of the carriage would be needed.

I ran into the house, brought out two Indian woven baskets from the back room, raced up the stairs, and began to fill the first one. I put in my second best summer petticoat, since I was wearing my best one, and two summer chemises, and stockings and my other pair of shoes. I filled the second basket with you, my dear book, with Elizabeth, the poetry book my grandfather gave me, the Pilgrim's Progress, the Bible that I received when I was eleven, and my second best bonnet.

I heard Mother say to Ruth, "Pack food for a long journey,"

141

Mother came upstairs with baskets of her own. When she saw my packing, she added a winter petticoat and a heavy shawl to the first basket and emptied my second basket entirely, saying we could take only what was most needed. She took away the basket and I saw it later filled with trenchers and spoons, the skillet and a kettle and pan. I put you in the bottom of the first basket.

For a long trip, there was room for four in the carriage, so Stacy and Ruth could not come with us. Father said we would leave them and Tobey at Uncle John's. I begged to take Tobey. Father said he could not stay in inns and we knew not where we would be and how a dog would fare. Father and Mother and Dudley sat in the front, and Ruth and Stacy and I in the back, and Tobey jumped in upon my lap, panting and excited to go for a ride.

As we set out, there were still people watching and pointing at us from around the Meeting House. A small number were gathered in front of our house, and I heard one shout at us, though I could not make out what was said. We turned into the Boston Way, my father whipping Hector, with the smell of Hector and the damp carriage about me, and the feeling of the best pewter wedged against my feet and Tobey slobbering on my best petticoat. Mother said to comfort us that our things would await us when we returned. I thought there was little certainty in her voice, and I said goodbye in my mind to Elizabeth with her yellow hair, and Molly the pig, and the Rose of Sharon.

As we drove further along, I felt still sadder. Polly and her mother and her aunt and Hannah's mother might be dead in a few weeks' time. I might never see Job or Hannah again. Even Sarah Abbot seemed dear.

As we drove into Uncle John's yard, there was no sign of him. We got out of the carriage. Ruth hugged me as tightly as the day I came back from running away with Polly. She whispered to me that she felt like she were losing her own child all over again. Stacy nodded goodbye to me, and I thought he looked unhappy, probably not because of leaving us but because Uncle John will put him to work in the fields. Father headed toward the house with them.

Tobey whined and circled. However we hugged and said good-bye and however Father called him, he would not leave me. Finally I went with him to the house and left him within. We had never been parted like this before. He whined and cried while I wished I could whine and cry. I did not, because I wished Tobey not to fear, but tears sprang to my eyes the instant I left the house.

Father explained our flight to Aunt Sally, and we were off again, through the air still damp from the morning rain.

We turned toward the North, and bumped along. The ruts in the roads had hardened in the drought, with the rain not enough to soften them. When the ruts did not match the width of the carriage, it felt like we should be thrown right out. I had to hold on to the pewter many times to prevent it being spilled upon the road. "Faster, Hector, faster," I kept thinking. Anyone following on horseback rather than a carriage would catch us in no time.

"Shall we be chased, Father, think you?" Dudley said, echoing my fear.

"Perhaps," Father said. "Certainly there shall be a warrant for my arrest. They shall have to go to Salem for it, however. We have a good head start."

Dudley said he was reminded of John Willard, the constable from Salem, who was hung the day Dudley went to Salem. He refused to arrest witches and was accused himself, escaped but was chased and caught.

Father said, "John Willard did not run until he found out they had the warrant, so he did not have our start. I despair of the legal system in dealing with Witchcraft, yet there are still a few protections it affords."

Father had never been so frank before about his disappointment with the law.

Since Dudley had begun, I thought I could ask, "Where shall we go?"

Father said Grandfather had friends in New Hampshire, and we would go there. When I said to Dudley that I had never been out of Massachusetts before, he said New Hampshire until most recently had been part of Massachusetts, so it was not so great a thing. It still felt like an adventure.

I felt sick in the pit of my stomach as I kept looking sideways around the carriage to see if there was the dust of horsemen coming from behind. I prayed mightily for our deliverance, and when I glanced at Mother, I often noted her eyes shut and her lips moving.

We rode further than I had ever gone before. Dudley was allowed to take the reins at times. It seemed hours since anyone had spoken. Then Dudley said in a strained voice,

"I am sorry I shall not go to Harvard tomorrow and I am afraid of what may happen to us. Whatever happens, I am proud to be your son."

I said Dudley had spoken truth, and I was proud to be Father's daughter. I had never said such a thing before.

Mother said, "I have always been proud to be your wife, but in all our life together, this is the moment I am most proud." Mother sounded like she would cry.

Father did not speak for some time, and I think he was embarrassed at our words. Then he said,

"I tried hard to find another way, but there was none. We should have left before."

Further north it had not rained and the dust was wicked. I wished we had changed into our older clothes, as my petticoat and chemise were so black I doubted they would ever be clean again. After we had gone for hours and hours, I had a sudden thought and said to Mother,

"I have forgotten my sampler."

She began to laugh, and I was startled. When her laughter turned to tears I was more startled. To calm her, I said I would start anew on a sampler. She said with more laughter and tears that I need not, and she put her arm about me and said,

"Maggie, you are a good girl."

I am pleased never to return to needle-work, but I do not understand Mother well. I cannot recall another time she has put her arm about me, other than when I came home from the forest.

Seventh of September, still later

We drove until it was well and truly dark. Hector's pace had become so slow that Dudley and I got out and walked along, as it made less weight for Hector to pull. When we finally arrived in Pentucket, I no longer felt excited or afraid, but only weary and hungry. Father said there was an inn here, and we found it after asking several folk. It had no sign, and was but a large house.

Having never been to an inn, I knew not what to expect. When we knocked upon the door, a fat man with a dirty gray apron appeared. I was startled to hear Father introduce himself as Douglas Bradbury of Topsfield, and I almost interrupted him before I understood what he was doing.

The innkeeper gestured to us to come in. I was disappointed to see that the front room, the tavern, was dark and dirty. A man sat at a stool drinking a tall glass of ale by a pale lantern light. When he turned to us and smiled I could see that most of his front teeth were gone. The one window in the room had been boarded up. The innkeeper saw me looking at the boards and he said,

"Twas a brawl t'other night."

Father asked if we might have a private room, and the innkeeper said

"None such. Women in one room, men in t'other."

He spoke as though he did not want to spend the words. A room for Mother and me and one for Dudley and Father did not sound so ill to me until I saw the rooms. Each had nothing but one large mattress to sleep upon for as many as should come. There was no room for our belongings, nor were there windows. The rooms smelled, the men's, where the odor of vomit was strong, especially.

Mother was very pale, but she knew as I did that there was no other place to go. The innkeeper saw her expression, and said,

"Women should have room to selves. Expect no others tonight."

After we had returned downstairs and Father was paying, I know not how much, the innkeeper inquired,

"Dinner?"

We agreed, though with little warmth. Father and Dudley had to care for Hector by themselves, and they carried our wares into the innkeeper's back room.

The tavern dinner was a mangy affair of pease porridge, thin and gray, with small bits of greasy ham in it. We ate it greedily, while the man with the few teeth at the bar came to the table to engage Father in conversation.

"Douglas Bradbury from Topsfield, eh? I used to come from there, yet I know you not. Where do you live?"

Father said he had not lived there long, and asked when the toothless one had lived there, which I thought was clever. Fortunately the man had not been there for a year. Father then spun a story about how we had moved there from Boston, and provided us with a new home on the outskirts of town. I was surprised at how easily he lied, and I wondered whether I have taken this ability from him. When the man asked about people in the town, Father knew them, because of Uncle John, and was able to tell the gossip about them.

I have had sleepless nights from worry, and the night upon the bank of Cochichewick Creek with Polly was the most frightening I have yet spent, yet I would trade any of them for that night in the Pentucket Inn. We put out the candle and lay down on the filthy mattress, and in a minute were covered with all manner of creatures— fleas and lice and something else. Mother stumbled into the hall to relight the candle. When she brought it back into the room, I could see a stream of light brown bedbugs creeping toward me out from the mattress and the wall in so large a number that I cried out as a sheep might bleat when surrounded by a circle of wolves. Their bites did not hurt but it was horrid to find them crawling on me. We tried sleeping upon the floor, and leaving the candle burning, but with little better result. We comforted ourselves that we would sleep in the carriage the next day. When I finally did fall off for a time upon the floor, I was wakened by a large mouse running over my arm.

In the morning Dudley told me their experience was the same with the bedbugs. In addition, the man from Topsfield came up drunk, would not sleep and asked many more questions about our family. Where we were headed? Why had we left Topsfield? Why we had set out on a journey in fine clothes? Father got us out early while the man still slept. It was a narrow escape.

Eighth of September

I was so glad to crawl into the carriage and leave that foul inn. I soon found we had not escaped so easily, as we had brought away lice and fleas, and the bedbug bites were fearsome. I itched and scratched until I drew blood. Since we had found no rest the night before, we took turns sleeping in the back of the carriage while one person walked.

We drove sometimes for an hour without seeing a house or another carriage. As the road became narrower, when we did meet another carriage, one would have to pull off the road to let the other pass. I felt safer, and I looked less often to see if any followed us.

When Mother was lying in back, and Dudley and I were walking, I saw her rummaging about our things. She sat up and gasped, "The pewter flagon has been stolen."

Father turned around from the driving and gave her a long look. Mother bowed her head and said out loud a prayer of thankfulness for our lives. I also said a silent prayer for us, for Polly, her family, Hannah's mother, and for Tobey, who I hoped would be safe at Uncle John's.

Finally we saw a board by the side of the road that said "New Hampshire." "Are we almost there?" I could not help but ask. Father shook his head wearily, and said we would have another night in an inn.

I tried to watch for animals. What I liked best was two baby foxes playing by the side of the road. They were small and red, and they reminded me of Tobey as they jumped about and chased each other. As the sun grew low in the sky, there were many animals—flocks of deer grazing, wild turkeys, a raccoon and a family of groundhogs.

This night's inn was better than the last. We had a private room for the four of us, and we all shared the bed. The fleas and lice bothered us, but there were no bedbugs. We met no one who knew Topsfield or who seemed interested in us.

The next day, we drove and drove. Dudley asked Father if we should stay at another inn, and Father said there were no more inns, and we should have to drive all the way. The time passed slowly. I no longer took interest in the animals, though Dudley said he saw a wolf at the side of a clearing.

We all smelled by then. Everyone except the driver had to walk, even Mother, as Hector is not used to pulling such a heavy load, especially for such a long time. I was allowed to drive, though Mother said it was unmaidenly. I had never done it before, and Dudley said that I was tolerably good at it.

It was most hot again, and it was hard to be comfortable either in or out of the carriage. While we were walking the sun was always shining on our backs so that we each had a bright red neck. Sweat formed like prickles on my back and then rolled down. It made the bites from the vermin itch worse than when I have poison ivy.

I was so weary I could hardly move one foot in front of the other. Our tempers were short, and Dudley and I growled at each other as we used to.

There were no more road markings. When we came to turnings, Father stopped the carriage to take a paper from his pocket and consult it. We went left and right and left again. The sun began to sink, and it was no longer hot, but it was hard to see the way. Once we had to retrace our steps. Mother groaned, "What if we are lost in the forest all night?"

Finally Father took a narrow track off to the right. In less than a mile we saw smoke rising from a chimney. One more bend and against the reddish gray of the evening sky, we could see the outlines of a dilapidated little house with a large barn. Mother's face looked bleak. We had arrived.

Eleventh of September

After living in a town, we are now a mile from the next farm, five miles from a village, and twelve miles from the sea. We shall probably not ever go to the sea, though I should love to, as I have only seen the sea once when we went to Boston.

Goody Hanover is a small brisk woman with a kind heart, who heated buckets upon buckets of water for us that first night, until the whole house was full of steam. She and her husband had heard that we might come. I see Father must have had it in his mind for some time that we should have to leave.

We spent hours combing the lice and nits out of our hair, though not that first night, when we fell exhausted into our beds in the Hanover's outbuilding. This little house is much like the one where Ruth and Stacy lived at the back of our old house. It brought them to mind, and also Tobey, who I hope is doing well. It is also like Polly's old home, without windows, and with a dirt floor. I think of what her life must have been like, as I grope about in the dark. It is probably just as dark in the jail.

Sixteenth of September

Life here is mainly chores to care for ourselves. The Hanovers must work hard to farm their property, with only two hired hands. Father and Dudley are out in the field each day at dawn to help with the harvest. Mother and I go to the house to help Goody Hanover, with many cooking and cleaning tasks.

Since there is no one here my age, my thoughts turn always to home. I wonder about those I know in the prison, Polly and her mother and aunt, and Hannah's mother, Reverend Dane's Joseph and the others. Sometimes I imagine them as they were, Polly's mother laughing loudly and speaking her mind, Eunice Frye gossiping, and Goody Ffaulkner wrapping her rose shawl about herself and looking grand. Then I think they are likely all changed, sitting there wordless and fearful. I think they are all in the same room, crowded upon a few benches, or sitting upon the floor, leaning upon each other with not enough room to sleep. It might be like our night in the Pentucket Inn, living in that dark room with the vermin, only with others crowded about. I wonder what they say to each other. Does Polly find comfort in her mother and aunt? How do they explain their confessions when they know they are not guilty? Do they think of death?

Father says that the court has just begun its fall session, and that some may be undergoing trials right now. I wonder if there were more arrests, and if there is a warrant out for our arrest.

I think also about Job. I wonder how he can abide living in the same house with Martha and to know his relations have been shut in prison by her doing. How do they speak to each other? I wonder if Job thinks about me.

Eighteenth of September

We have spent two days picking most of the apples. They are a different kind than at home, smaller and tarter and more likely to have worm holes. They taste fine and the picking was a pleasure. Mother said I am too old now to climb the ladders to fetch the high fruit. I did it regardless when she was not around.

Dudley did not tell tales on me for climbing the ladder, and we spend more time together than of old. He pines upon Harvard, though he does not speak of it to Father. I tell him that when we go home, surely we will go home, then he can enter. He has more time to learn before he goes. Sadly there are few books for him to read in this home. At night we read aloud to each other from old familiar ones like Pilgrim's Progress, taking turns until the candle light makes our eyes ache.

Twentieth of September

We have so many apples, and I have taken to making all the pies. Goody Hanover says they are as good as any she has eaten. Mother tells her she must not say things that will go to my head.

Twenty third of September

Today I was out gathering mint to dry before it freezes, and admiring the red color of the maple trees, which is even finer than at home. I was returning to the house with my arms laden, when I heard a horse upon the road. A familiar voice cried out,

"Maggie, mine own sweet niece!" and there was Uncle John.

After he dismounted and we embraced, he took me up behind him, mint and all, and we rode to the house. When we reached the house, and all had embraced, and we had congratulated each other upon our health, I saw Uncle John's happiness abate.

"There is some good news," he said slowly. "Some who were taken that day at the Meeting House have been released. The Tyler family, and Reverend Dane's Joseph."

"Not Hannah's mother?" I asked.

"No, she stays in prison. That is little good news to balance the bad I have for all of you," he said. "Perhaps especially for Maggie."

"Is it Polly?" My throat was dry.

"Polly is still in prison," he said. "She has not been tried."

"Tell all, from the beginning," said Father.

He told us there was indeed a warrant for Father's arrest, and for Mother's as well. They have been accused of killing nine persons. We children had not been charged.

"That would come later," Father said.

Uncle John thought that no one had pursued us, as they knew not where we had gone after leaving his place. They had guessed, however, from knowing Father and from watching the carriage, that we had gone to see Uncle John first.

Father said, "I fear we have brought trouble upon your head."

"They did not come to see me at once, but after a few days. Talk festered in the village. Constable Ballard came to see me, and inquired where you had gone, and I said in truth that I had not been here upon your arrival."

"On the seventeenth, the trials resumed. Poor old Ann Foster was condemned to death, as was Abigail Ffaulkner. In spite of all Reverend Dane's influence upon his daughter, Abigail at last confessed. She shall be executed but they shall wait until after the birth of her child."

Father and Mother looked sorely grieved. Goody Ffaulkner was their friend, and they no doubt felt about her as I would about Polly.

Uncle John went on, "Also Samuel Wardwell was condemned. They allowed Martha Sprague to testify to all the harm he did to her. He no doubt rued the fun he had with fortune-telling as they placed the noose around his neck. The hanging was scheduled for yesterday."

I shivered at the thought, and remembered Dudley's description of the hangings. Probably Polly and her mother and aunt and Hannah's mother yesterday were sitting on the dark crowded benches and heard Samuel Wardwell being brought out for the gallows. The men must be in a separate cell, yet close enough for the women to hear.

Three days ago Uncle John received a message from Captain Osgood. Since his daughter was taken, as well as his brother's wife and his manservant, Captain Osgood has become a true friend to Reverend Dane, and is doing all he can against the Witchcraft trials. He knows what is going to happen in the town, as he still has many friends among the selectmen.

Captain Osgood's message said,

"John, you must flee. I trust your family shall be safe, and if there is danger to them I shall take them away myself."

John told us that he had not wished to flee before he had to, as the harvest was in progress, and he feared it would be lost without him. He prepared a day's supply of provisions, and left it by his horse and saddle, ready to go if needed.

"I was working in the field when a hand came out to tell me that Constable Ballard's carriage was in the yard. He was not alone, but there was another carriage behind, with Martha Sprague and her friends."

"I ran to the outbuilding where my horse was waiting. I saddled her up, and led her through the trees up the ridge so I would not be seen. From the top of the ridge I saw the crowd descend upon the house, like ants onto honey. Many had guns out. Tobey came barking at them and snapping, and after someone hit him with a stick, he bit her. Sally came out of the house, protesting, and they let her be. But they scooped up Tobey, muzzling him with a rope, and they carried him away."

"What has happened to him?" I asked. My mouth was so dry it was hard to get the words out. This was the bad news. I knew.

"I know not how to tell you, Maggie. The first night out I made it as far as Pentucket. All were talking there at the inn that the day before a dog had been hung at Andover by an angry crowd who thought it to have been bewitched by John Bradstreet. I did not tell my real name at the inn, thank the Lord."

I could not understand it at first. The dog must be Tobey, it could be no other. Hung. How does one hang a dog? I shivered, and then I began to weep. I know not how long I wept, and none could comfort me.

Mother tells me it is nothing compared to the loss of a child, and I see better how she grieves still for Annie. Father tells me to think on how the Carrier children felt to see their mother hung. Dudley says little, but he pushes the best food upon our trencher toward me.

I have wept a good deal this summer, but never so much as now. I weep for my dog more than any. Tis my own heart and I cannot account for it.

First of October

Yesterday the hired hands slaughtered a pig for the winter. I stayed in the house, but the scream pierced me and I could not stop thinking about it as I fell asleep. I dreamed that I had traveled to Gallows Hill, as Dudley had done, and that the cart with the condemned came forth and upon it were Tobey and a pig which was our own Molly. The Reverend Barnard was on a horse and he spit high into the air on the "s's" saying,

"These are witches of the worst."

Tobey was wagging his tail as they placed the noose about his neck. I was in the crowd trying to run forward to save him, screaming and not able to move. I awoke with a strange sound in my throat, which woke Dudley.

Twenty first of October

I have left off writing. I have no heart for anything. Today a letter arrived, forwarded by Grandfather. This is not the first letter he has forwarded, but I had no curiosity about the ones before.

I am copying today's letter, from Job Tyler, addressed to Dudley, into you.

155

Fifteenth of October, year of our Lord 1692

My dear Dudley,

I think often about you and your family and hope for your health and safety. I have been told by Reverend Dane that should I write to your Grandfather, he would forward it, and I hope you shall receive this missive and my good wishes.

I know not what news you have received, and I think you must know this, but I shall tell it again in case. I was not there, but have heard fully from several who were. When the crowd came, armed and angry, to arrest your uncle, they were angrier yet to find him not at home. They came upon Tobey, who was protecting the house. Martha Sprague waved a stick at him, then hit him hard on the back. He bit her under her skirts on the ankle. Martha began to shriek, "Witch! Witch! He has been bewitched!"

Henry Chandler, who is sweet on Martha, spoke to the others and they picked up Tobey, muzzled him and took him away in their own carriage, to be charged. What role Constable Ballard played I do not know.

On the way back, Tobey managed to free himself from his restraints, and he tried to bite Martha again. Martha began to scream and rant and all in the carriage were incensed. They stopped upon the way back at Woodchuck Hill and hung Tobey from a tree.

The next day, the town could talk of nothing else. "Did you hear, they hung the Bradstreets' dog for a Witch?" It went around and around. Folk said, "What think you, how remarkable that Tobey, who seemed a good dog, could be a Familiar of Satan?"

I could not abide that Tobey should hang there on Woodchuck Hill for passersby to see, and I told my father that I wished to take the wagon to cut him down. Father tried to prevent me, and Martha and her mother were wrathful. I went regardless.

I do not think that Tobey suffered, for his neck was broken clean. I was angered to see him, as well as sorrowful. Instead of coming straight,

I drove around the town at a slow pace before coming back into the village. Then I buried Tobey in your yard, under the elm tree in the front, for all eyes to see. Reverend Barnard came out of his house and told me I should not but I ignored him, and he went away. It took a time, as I dug a hole three feet deep, so no animals shall disturb his rest. I thought what Maggie would like, and I cut a branch from the Rose of Sharon to place upon him. Several folk gathered to watch and mutter. Reverend Dane came by and said, loudly, that it was right that Tobey should have a decent burial.

By the time I went to Peters' store the next day, the talk had changed. When I came up, Andrew Peters was saying, "How could folk be so witless as to suppose that good dog was a familiar of Satan?" All were agreeing, and blaming Martha and the others who hung him. It was like the way the wind shifts in a nor'easter. Who can honor the doings of folk who would hang a dog?

Other things have occurred to help. People have been saying in private that they do not think that your father and mother could be Witches, that many in the prison could not be Witches, and they have asked why all Reverend Dane's family has been taken. Also, the fall rains came, some crops were saved, and it looks no longer that we shall starve. One other thing of import has occurred. One of the women testified that it was Reverend Barnard himself who told her daughter the words to use when casting spells. I trust that has shaken the Reverend's faith in spectral evidence. I have heard that Reverend Cotton Mather has also revised his view of spectral evidence.

At all events, a letter was written to the Salem court requesting leniency for some of those taken. Many signed, including the Reverend Barnard.

The good news is that today many have been released on bail, mainly children. These include the children of Martha Carrier, and several other children, and best news of all, for me and for Maggie, Polly Bridges!

Our family shall take Polly in and care for her. I shall send news

157

of her after I see her. Please give my regards to all your family, and be sure to give this news to Maggie. I know you all, and Maggie especially, grieve for Tobey. I believe Tobey has helped to play a role in the sea change in our town, and perhaps it could be a comfort to think that he died in a worthy cause. Like a small soldier, perhaps.

With humble respects,
Job Tyler

I was in a delight that Polly was released, and that Job wrote. His letter is written to Dudley, yet I know he thought of me.

He has come closest to comforting me.

First of November

We sat at our own small board today, without the Hanovers and the help, as they were all plowing the fields under. It felt warm, though the day was chill. We seldom mention home when the Hanovers are about. We had just begun to pass the skirret stew when there was a knock upon the door, and a traveler came with a letter. Father said,

"It is from my father," and he began to read it as the rest of us ate the stew.

When he finished, he said with a smile, "Things are changing back at home," and began to read aloud portions of the letter.

Governor Phipps has forbidden any new trials and the use of spectral evidence in trials. He has dissolved the court that was trying the Witches.

Father said, "All the evidence against us is spectral only," and after a pause he added, "Perhaps we shall return soon!"

Tis turning colder, and the weather here is even rawer than it is at home. We have had five days of storm, with not a sign of sun, and rain so high it has come over the threshold into our poor house. With our dirt floors turned to mud, and Uncle John here, the building is even less comfortable. Today as I made the pumpkin soup for dinner, there were flurries of snow. I long for home.

Fifth of December

We are going home! Father received a letter from Reverend Barnard asking him to return, saying that no one should harm him. Many in town want Father to draft a letter that all shall sign to the Salem court asking for the release of the prisoners. Dudley has received another letter from Job. In it, he asked for my health in particular, and said that all in town wish for our return.

Seventh of December

Mother says that trips home are shorter than the same distance gone away from home. I think not. In the cold, the road went on forever and seemed like it would never end. Last night we spent in Pentucket again, with the same vermin, which were slightly less lively because of the temperature. Mother and I were never warm though we spent the night back to back for comfort.

In the carriage we huddled together with all our clothes about us to keep warm. It is good to have the sun at our face on this trip.

It is more crowded with Uncle John, and we must walk even more. Dudley and Mother have both caught the grippe.

Eighth of December

Home, home, home! So much to write! As our carriage met the road from Salem, we saw the dust of another carriage and then the carriage and then in a minute knew it to be Hannah's family. They were coming from Salem, bearing Hannah's mother home. She has been released! We jumped down, and Hannah embraced me before I could tell her to beware of nits. I have never seen her so in a pleasure, with restraint gone from her manner. She said,

"I have my mother back, and now you too!"

Then I turned to look at her mother, and I almost cried out. I would have thought her to be Hannah's grandmother, she seemed so aged. Her hair had turned gray all through, and her face was lined as deep as the creek bed in the summer drought. I saw then that I need not have said anything about nits, as I could see many small white bodies against the thin gray hair at the front of her bonnet, which was so foul and matted it had no strings and lay askew upon her head. In spite of all, her face had such a smile of pleasure upon it, and she kept her arm about Hannah so, that I felt that this must be how folk feel at the gate of Heaven.

I felt a pang that were it Mother and I, separated and reunited, we should not find such emotions to lie within us.

Hannah's mother thanked me many times over for saving her daughter on the day of the Touch Test, and said that however her suffering, she counted herself blessed that her children were spared.

We left the Danes, and in a short time pulled into our yard. I felt delight, though everything seemed smaller and shabbier than I had remembered. I had to stifle a cry when I spied the fresh dug earth in front of the elm tree. While I was away, it was easy to forget and think that Tobey was back at home and that I would see him again.

Uncle John had brought the animals to his farm soon after we left, so there were none about. The yard seemed strange and quiet. As we went through the house, I heard Mother said to Father, "It appears that little has been stolen."

Father said, "Even without the watchful eye of Eunice Frye," and Mother said he was a poet as fine as his mother.

It was wondrous to climb to the loft and open my chest and see my clothes still there. I was too foul to put them on until I washed so I drew water from the pump and brought it within, though the fire had barely started to warm the house. I scrubbed myself with a rag, shivering in the cold. Then I took a deep breath and thrust my head into the bucket for my hair. The lye in the soap made my head sting, and I hoped it was killing lice and nits as well. Afterwards, I combed out as many as I could, knowing that Mother would help me with it later. I dried my hair as best as I could, hurrying through all, as I wanted to go see Polly. I dressed in my winter petticoat, put my heavy green shawl upon my shoulders, and left the house without asking permission.

I turned right, remembered that Polly was at Tyler's, and turned about. I ran all the way. I thought that of old Tobey would be running at my side.

As I came around the bend, my heart leapt up to see Polly in the yard. She was minding the children, sitting on a stump, with piles of large gray stockings in her lap as she mended. I ran to her and she jumped up, spilling the stockings heedlessly, and we embraced. Mehitable saw me also, and came running, and put her arms about me from behind my knees, and pulled Polly and me apart.

Then I saw it was not Polly. She was all changed. Twas not so much her appearance, though she did indeed look older and she did not look well. Her hair was stringy, and her skin was red and chapped, with the freckles standing out upon it angrily. Mostly it was her manner. It was as though I was talking to one of Mother's friends. She was sober and careful and not plain spoken in any way. She would not talk of her time in the jail other than to say it was detestable beyond words. She would not speak of her mother or aunt who were held there still. She reminded me that she is but on bail, and must go back to face trial. Her face turned pale as she said this.

"Martha shall no doubt testify against me."

I had thought that coming home would take away her burden of suffering, but I realize she is still in prison, there with her mother and her aunt. Perhaps all her trials shall be done with in a time, yet I cannot imagine ever again going into the forest with her for fun. As I write this, I realize I have not played in months, and I felt a pang that perhaps I am more sober and grown up as well. I do not want either Polly or me to be grown up.

I asked Polly for Job's health, and she looked at me strangely. I realize that although I have never spoke to her of my feelings for Job, she knew that Job had buried Tobey and that it was in some part for me. Perhaps she could also tell something from my voice. She knows me better than any other. She spoke for the first time plainly. She said,

"He is well. Do you wish him to court you? Who, think you, shall come courting for me, who has been to jail as a Witch?"

I wanted to embrace her again, but felt she did not wish it. She seemed almost angry at me. I know she was pleased to see me. I think it is that I have no compass for her pain. I left soon after.

As I walked down the road so much more slowly than I had arrived, Job came up upon the same auburn horse that had thrown Martha some months before. He jumped from the horse to greet me, but the horse pulled and demanded his attention, and he could not speak to me for a moment. I thanked him for his care for Tobey, and his care for Polly. He spoke to me gravely that he had missed our family, and not Dudley alone, and that he hoped to call upon us often. As he left, he touched my hand, which was cold. His fingers were cold also, and yet that spot upon my skin feels warm now even as I write.

My thoughts are in a muddle. I have longed for home for so long, and now I am here it is not as I imagined. I miss Tobey, I am both so pleased and sorry for Hannah's mother, I am so sad for Polly and I am so glad for Job.

Ninth of December

Today we went to pick up Ruth and Stacy and the animals from Uncle John's. We drove over in our carriage, and returned in Uncle John's wagon.

Ruth gave me a fearsome embrace, and exclaimed that I had grown in but a few months. Adults always say that about younger folk.

Stacy had little to say, and his breath smelled of drink. Uncle John said that his servants and hired hands had complained that Stacy had not pulled his weight.

I think none of the animals but Molly recognized me. She thrust her face into mine and grunted. I remembered my dream about her and Tobey, and I missed Tobey.

Fourteenth of December

The Sabbath, and much is changed! Everyone has returned to Reverend Dane's service. Our voices rang out when we sang the psalms, and my own wavery high notes could no longer be heard above the general din. Reverend Dane spoke from the pulpit of his pleasure in our return, and of the release of Hannah's mother and also his daughter Goody Ffaulkner. Goody Ffaulkner looked less worn than Hannah's mother, perhaps because she is with child and so is plump. Her face is thin, however. She sat most still, without any fancy clothes. She wore a simple shawl of brown wool wrapped tightly about her. Her head was bowed and she had not her former straight back or look of pride. Reverend Dane also offered up a prayer for the release of others held unjustly, and I knew he thought of his daughter Elizabeth and his granddaughter Elizabeth.

Between the services all brought food to share and welcomed us and the others home. It was cold, but the sun shone mightily. Hannah and Sarah told me much of what has happened while we were away. It seemed we had been gone so long, and yet some things changed not at all. Hannah has just finished the same gray afghan she had begun to knit the day we went to see Goody Carrier arrested. When I said that I should not have to return to my sampler, Sarah laughed and Hannah's arched face looked pained for me. Hannah does not understand how I feel about needle work. Mother has been true to her word, and has not pushed me to the needle. I have taken on much more of the cooking since we have been away as I learned many useful recipes from Goody Hanover.

I spoke only in passing to Polly, as she seemed to avoid me. Job was there, but did not speak to me.

In the afternoon, the Reverend Barnard spoke not a word about Witches, and also welcomed us and those released back to Andover.

Eunice Frye was released on bail today. When her nephew helped her from the carriage, she seemed as stiff and old as Goody Foster. Her black petticoats that were once so fine had that greasy faded look, like what you would see on a tramp who has never washed his clothes. Her bonnet and clothes were as ragged as Hannah's mother's had been.

Mother and I walked across the yard to greet her, and her nephew asked if we could help her get settled, as he had something important to attend to. He looked like he was handling a snake, he held her arm at such a distance. I wondered if he was afraid of her. Eunice smelled as though she had been sick in her clothes, and we had to help her into her house, one on either elbow. Her face was blank and child-like. She seemed not to know us, or to know where she was. She called me Marnie, which I think is her sister's name. I could not fathom my sharp-tongued neighbor so lost.

After we brought her into her house, I fetched wood to start the fire. Mother went back to the house and prepared a drink of whiskey in hot milk to warm her. Then Mother said that she must return home to prepare the noon meal, and I should stay with Eunice. I offered to prepare the meal, but Mother shook her head.

There were still some things in her larder, but the mice had made their way into most of it. I said I would go to Peters' to fetch for her. She began to weep, to clutch at my arm, and to beg me to stay with her. I said I would not leave her, but she kept gripping my arm and calling me Marnie. At last I was able to pull her toward the fire, sit her down and cover her with a blanket. I made some samp and fed it to her as though she was an infant. She fell asleep in the chair, snoring louder than Dudley. When I went home, Mother sent Stacy to sit with her.

When she awoke and saw Stacy, we could hear the screams from our house. I suppose she did not recognize him. Then Ruth went over, and bathed her a bit and put her into bed.

Who shall care for her? No one wants to, it seems. There is something fearful about that absent moon face.

Twenty first of December

Father has spoken to Eunice's nephews in the neighborhood, and they agreed to help care for her. We still take turns minding her.

Twenty third of December

Why has Job not come to see us?

Twenty fifth of December

Tis Christmas today, and it snowed, that lovely wet snow that dresses the trees and houses in white. We walked across the way to the Meeting House for special prayers. I was looking about me all in a wonder so that I did not watch my feet, and I stepped right into a puddle. My feet were so wet and cold during the service that I longed to take my shoes off and rub the feeling back into them.

Before he began, Reverend Dane announced,

"Ann Foster has died today in the prison."

A gasp went through the meeting house. He said it was a

misfortune to her that her husband had lived so long, as that had fueled the talk of her Witchery. Though she had been accused so early and condemned to death, yet there were doubts about her guilt that had prevented her being executed. He said it was a sign she was not a Witch that she should die on Christ's birthday.

When it was his turn, Reverend Barnard spoke of the corrupt practices in other lands to celebrate Christ's birthday—feasting, drinking and giving of gifts. Some even fell a tree and place candles upon it and dance about it. He then spoke of how we had left England to practice our belief more purely. I knew this, of course, except for the part about the tree. As I sat there with my feet without feeling, I wished for a giant roaring fire and a feast roasting upon it, perhaps a stew of pork cooking in hot apple cider, with chestnuts popping at the side, and some lovely gift waiting for me. I could even see the sparkles of the candles upon the tree. I shall pray to be better, yet I fear I shall always be a poor Puritan. I no longer fear that I am a Witch.

Third of January, Year of Our Lord 1693

Job came to dinner last night, as Dudley leaves for Harvard tomorrow. They said they would take him now at the start of the second term. I made an apple pie with apples stored from the fall at Uncle John's. Job said it was most tasty even before he knew twas I who made it. Tis good fortune that Aunt Sarah stayed at Uncle John's so that she could supervise the harvest and that they have been so generous to us.

It was the first time I have seen Job to speak to in spite of what he said the day I returned. I have thought about it each day. Perhaps he feels awkward visiting in front of Dudley. Tonight he and Dudley included me in their talk after the dinner. They both say that no one in town talks of Witchcraft now, other than to wonder when folks will be returned, and to marvel that so many were taken. They say tis clear no new folk will be accused, and that the others shall be returned. I hope they are right.

Fourth of January

Dudley left for Harvard today. Stacy drove the carriage around to the front and Hector stood there stomping and snorting huge plumes of breath like smoke. It was time for Dudley to get into the carriage with his chest of clothes and books, and I was amazed when tears began to well from my eyes. I was also amazed to see a slight wetness in Dudley's own eyes as we embraced. Mother had no tears, but bit her lip greatly, and as soon as he was gone, she looked at me and said,

"Mind you clean the oven out today,"
and then ran up the stairs to her room and I could hear her weeping for an hour. I could hear her thought as clear as though it were spoken,

"Now I am left with only one, and she the least of all three to my liking."

Twelfth of January

I noted when I entered the Meeting House today that none of the Tylers nor Polly were there. I soon saw the reason, as Reverend Dane made several announcements from the pulpit today.

"Goodwoman Mary Bridges has been tried for a Witch and found not guilty."

168

I almost leapt up from the bench. Polly's mother would be coming home! They had gone to get her! Then Reverend Dane went on,

"Miz Mary Post has been tried for a Witch and found guilty and sentenced to death."

My heart sank. How could Polly's mother be found innocent and her aunt be found guilty? How can there be such good news and such dire together?

And then the third announcement.

"I am pleased to tell you that my daughter Goodwoman Elizabeth Johnson was tried for a Witch, found innocent, and was released a few days ago."

I looked about for her, and was surprised that she was not there.

And then the fourth announcement.

"Her daughter Elizabeth was tried for a Witch, found guilty, and condemned to death."

I saw why his daughter had not come, how could she leave her house if her own daughter had been condemned to death? There can be no joy when some come home and some are to die. Job and Dudley think the Witchcraft illness is over. Tis not over.

Thirteenth of January

After I cleared the breakfast things away, and had helped Ruth start the noon meal, I said to Mother,

"Goody Bridges returned home yesterday, and she will need many things. May I take her eggs?"

Mother agreed, and I counted myself clever, as if I had said merely that I was curious to visit Polly and her mother, I should have been refused. As I walked over, I found my heart beating heavily, and I hoped Polly's mother should not have lost her wits like Eunice Frye.

169

Eunice is doing better, and recognizes us now. She is still confused, but does not speak nonsense unless there is some mention of the jail, when she turns pale and begins to look absent again.

When I came into the Bridges' yard, my heart lifted up, for there was smoke in the chimney, the snow brushed off the path, and light through the chinks in the logs. The house looked already like it was home to somebody instead of the cold empty hovel it has lain for months.

I knocked with Goodman Bridges' handsome iron lion paw upon the door, and it opened. I was struck with the smell of soap and lye, and then taken about with Goody Bridges' strong clean arms.

"Thank you for the eggs," she said after the greeting. "Will you lend Polly a hand with the scrubbing, now?"

I have never scrubbed so gladly. After seeing Hannah's mother, and Eunice Frye, and knowing that Ann Foster had died from the conditions, it was a delight to see Polly's mother so unchanged. She is thinner, yet she grumbled and gossiped and worked, all together, just as hard as ever she had before. I learned all manner of things.

She said that old Ann Foster had been sick throughout, her pleurisy worse and worse till she could not breathe at all. She kept all awake at night with her gasping for air, and it was a wonder she had lasted as long as she had.

Elizabeth Dane was convicted because she confessed to everything. Elizabeth had become convinced that she was a Witch.

"Her grandfather may be a Reverend, yet Elizabeth is a poor ignorant fool. She even showed red spots on her body. 'Look,' said she. 'These have been sucked by evil spirits.'"

"How about your sister-in-law? Why was she convicted?" I ventured.

Polly's mother hmmphed and looked at me angrily.

"She should never have turned down Timothy Swan, though he is a poor specimen of a man for whom she cared not. Tis unjust, yet that was her undoing. No one trusts a thornback."

"She is in my prayers," I said.

We talked no more of the prison. As Goody Bridges swept out mouse droppings from the cupboard, and Polly and I scrubbed walls and the fireplace and the board, mostly in silence, the warm water and the lye reddening our hands, I felt something hard between me and Polly loosen a little.

Nineteenth of February

I am fourteen today. I received you a year ago, and it has been over a month since I have written in you. I thought I might receive another book for a gift but I did not. There are a few pages left within you.

Mother and Father gave me a fine bonnet from England with pink ribbon upon it, which sets nicely against my brown hair. It is the finest bonnet I have ever had.

Job came today while I made pies, and told me he had heard that Governor Phipps had sent to England for a general pardon for all left in the prison. Father said a prayer at the board this evening that the answer would come speedily.

While I was putting the pies in the oven, the kitchen all steamy from the stew on the fire, Job came into the room and reached into his pocket.

"I think it is your birthday," he said.

I began to weep when I saw it, a small carving that he had whittled from a block of birch wood. He had put blackening over it in some places, so it was a black and white dog, with all the markings correct, even the small white patch upon Tobey's head.

With that sign of Job's regard, I felt bold enough to ask him why he did not visit me for so long after our return, and tis only in the last month that he has come to call.

"Was it Dudley? Did you fear his teasing should you visit me?"

"Twas Polly," he said. "You cannot know what it was like while she lived in our house, without her mother, and with Martha there."

He said Polly had needed all his care, that he had not wanted to leave her to the abuse of Martha and the Hussy. I like it that Job calls his step-mother "The Hussy" also.

"Was Polly aggrieved with me?"

"Had I called upon you, she would have been. I was her only friend, and she would not have wanted to take a portion of me rather than the whole."

I felt hurt that Polly did not regard me as her friend and support at that time. Even though her father has come home also, and is not drinking, still we are not friends as we once were. I see Hannah more, and sometimes Sarah, and of course Job.

Ruth is supposed to stay in the room with us when Job visits yet she knows my heart and does not. When Job left, he took my hand for a moment, and held it tightly. I have such feelings. I wonder if they are sinful. I think not.

Seventh of April

I heard the news from Father, and went to Polly's at once. It was a fine sunny day, the first when I did not shiver beneath my shawl as I walked along. Polly's mother and father had gone to get Miz Post, and Polly was outside in the sun hoeing the garden for the new planting. The smell of new-turned earth was strong. Mehitable and the two others were playing about.

"Thank the Lord," I said to Polly. "Your life is restored."

She looked at me oddly.

"What do you mean?" she said.

"You have been released, your mother has been released, your father has come home, and now at last your aunt has been released! You can return to your life as it was before."

"Yes," said Polly, her voice very loud and cold. "I know that is what you think. You know nothing! You know nothing! What do you know of my nightmares, or of my mother's, or of Mehitable's? Mehitable cannot sleep through the night, without waking crying for her mother. I wake most nights myself, with visions of the jail, or of a noose hanging above my head. Have you forgotten that I have been released on bail, but not found innocent? You say you are my friend, yet you know nothing, nothing, nothing, of what my life was like in the jail, and after too, living with Martha and the Hussy. You could not help me and your father would not help me. Even the letters written to the court were about the gentlefolk of the town, not my sort of folk. There is no point in pretending, as we did when we were younger. We are separate, you and I, you with your fine house and bonnets, and I without. We are separate and we shall always be so."

I had never heard her in such a rage. I began to weep, and spoke through tears.

"I have tried to be your friend," I said. "I went to the forest with you, I tried to save you from the jail, I have thought of you and your suffering so many times and prayed for you so often. I know I have not suffered as you have, yet Father was accused himself, and we were forced to flee, and I know it is nothing, nothing to your suffering, yet I have lost Tobey in so cruel a manner. Can you not see how much I care . . ."

Here I began to weep in earnest, and then in a moment Polly as well.

I put my arms about her and we wept together.

I have not written in you of late. I have come near to the end of the pages, so I am writing smaller than my usual scrawl. I need you less. I speak more from my heart to others. Polly and I talk about everything. We go on no more adventures in the forest, yet we are closer than before.

Polly has told me that she confessed to end the terror of her examination, as well as more about the filth, the crowding, the heat and the cold in the jail. We talk also of our families. I have spoken more of my distance from Mother and the pain it causes me. I have always known that though Mother cares for me, she does not favor me as she does Dudley. Tis only as I have spoken it to Polly that I have truly known it. Tis a thing of hurt that shall not go away, yet it is eased in the telling.

Polly speaks to me of her father, and the pain of his drinking. He has hit her when in his cups. Tis hard for her to fathom it, as he is kind when he is sober, and she must fear him at times and love him at others. I count my blessings for my own father.

As I was writing, Father arrived home though it is still morning, to tell us the news. The general pardon has arrived from England! All remaining in the prison are released! Polly has been found not guilty! I shall run to her shortly, but I have just put the bread in the oven and must wait till it is browned.

Father and I then spoke of how Witchcraft still affects our town. I said I did not fathom how Martha Sprague can live here still, walking about, tossing her dark hair, as though she had done nothing. Folk treat Martha much as ever. And how do the Salem girls, like Ann, live with their conscience?

Father says there are wounds that heal and wounds that do not heal, and sometimes we cannot see the unhealed ones, as they are inside. I said I knew, from Polly. I said to him,

"You must not think Polly to be common. She has taught me much."

Father said he understood, and indeed he has not complained how much I see her, or how much I see Job.

Eunice Frye, however, is more herself, and she said to me, "Do your parents approve how much time you spend with that Tyler boy?"

I do spend much time with Job. We talk of anything and everything. I can tease him as Polly does on how he bites his nails when troubled, or how he lies upon the hearth instead of sitting properly, or how he eats an apple all around.

I think often of Tobey, when I pass under the elm tree in the front. Job tells me I must find me another dog. It shall be a long time before I am ready.

I feel sorrowful to say good-bye to you, my Book, as once you were my solace. I need you no more, but I bless you for being my true friend when there was none other.

Afterword

What Happened to Them

Maggie Bradstreet: She married Job, and they had six children, four girls and two boys. They named their first born, a boy, Dudley.

Job Tyler: He became a leader of the community, serving as constable and selectman and on a number of committees. He made grants of his land to the town.

Dudley Bradstreet (Maggie's father): He was never governor, but continued to hold a number of important offices in the town. He lost all his money late in life.

Dudley Bradstreet (Maggie's brother): He did graduate from Harvard and became a minister. After some time in Connecticut, he and his wife and children left the New World and he was ordained in the English church. The next month, at the age of thirty-six, he came down with small pox and died.

Reverend Francis Dane: He never stepped down from his position as minister in Andover. If there is any hero of the Andover story, it is he, as he never stopped preaching about "our sin of ignorance."

Reverend Thomas Barnard: He also continued to preach in Andover. His house and tombstone may be visited today in Andover.

Ann Putnam (the "pale girl" from Salem involved in the Touch Tests): People who saw her when she was "bewitched" hardly expected her to live. Fourteen years after the trials, she confessed at her church that she had sinned, saying it was a delusion of Satan that deceived her, rather than ill will. The congregation forgave her.

Stacy: The year after our story, Dudley Bradstreet lost, by drowning, "a mullato . . . named Stacy." Maggie's family's "servants" were African American slaves, like almost all the servants at the time. We tend not to think that slavery was practiced in the North, but it was. I would have liked Maggie to be more sensitive to the plight of Ruth and Stacy, but it wouldn't have been realistic for the time. Ruth is the only Andover resident whose name was not listed in the 1692 census, as names of "servants" were not generally included. I did try to give Ruth an opportunity to tell her story, and to show the culture as it was, complete with the Puritan belief that the Devil was a black man.

How the Story Came About

Before the era when the Internet provided help, my mother spent years traveling around and researching our family background, both hers and my father's. I thought it was pretty dull until my parents began to write up the stories about the ancestors. Here is my father's account of Dudley Bradstreet.

"Dudley Bradstreet, son of Simon and Anne, was Justice of the Peace in Andover. After granting thirty to forty warrants for witchcraft, he became disgusted with the situation and refused to issue any more. He and his wife were soon after accused of killing nine persons by witchcraft. They were forced to escape from the area. His brother, John, was then accused of afflicting a dog. He also fled. The dog was executed by the townspeople!"

Now there was a story! I found support for it from other documents. It seemed to me that the dog must have had some relationship to the Bradstreet family. Since it isn't mentioned as

John's dog, it would make sense if it belonged to Dudley's family, so that executing it would be a way of getting back at the Bradstreets.

As I found out more about the families, I was perplexed that Maggie Bradstreet had married Job Tyler. Job's stepsister, Martha Sprague, was the leader among the Andover girls in fingering the witches, and Maggie's father at the end combated the witchcraft craze, so wouldn't the families have been opposed to each other? Looking deeper, I noticed that three of Job's aunts were among the accused. There appeared to have been a split between the family members. In addition, one family among Job's relatives, the Bridges, lived only a short distance from Maggie, and one of them, Polly Bridges, was Maggie's age. Surely they must all have known each other well. The story I have told is not the only way it could have happened, but it is likely to be close to the truth.

All of the book's characters from Andover, except for Ruth, were real people, taken from the records of the time brought together by the Historical Societies of Andover and North Andover. I used nicknames for Margaret Bradstreet (Maggie) and Mary Bridges (Polly), as I thought it was too confusing to have a Margaret, Mary, and Martha as main characters.

Whenever I could, I used historical facts. The Peters had a store, Thomas Parker is listed as non compos mentis, and Timothy Swann's family ran the ferry and accused Polly's aunt of witchcraft. Martha Sprague accused several because of a fall from a horse. Maggie's father and Uncle John did stand in the stocks for drunkenness and shooting off their guns in the meeting house. The letters quoted in the story that Dudley wrote to the courts can be found in historical records.

Anne Dudley Bradstreet, Maggie's grandmother, was the first woman poet in America. Her early life is the subject of my next book.

About the Times

All Puritan women covered their heads with bonnets. Clothing was of dull "sad" colors, but there was less black worn than our popular conception. Women wore the "chemise," a floor length white shirt, at all times, to bed and under their outer clothes. It was the only underclothing worn. The quality of the chemise and whether it bore any decoration would depend on the amount of money and social standing the family bore. Petticoats were worn over the chemise, and piled on for warmth in the winter. It was acceptable to wear bright colored petticoats underneath. Clothes were usually washed once a month, and even well-off individuals seldom had more than two or three changes of clothing. People themselves seldom bathed.

Corn was the staple of the diet, and at every meal poor families ate "samp" (cornmeal ground—usually by the children—in a large mortar and pestle). Although we associate potatoes and tomatoes with the New World, Puritans did not eat them, fearing they were poisonous. They did eat a variety of other fruits and vegetables, especially beans. Cows and sheep were kept on the Commons, a far cry from the beautiful green expanses we see today in New England towns. Pigs were required to be fenced, yoked, and provided with rings so they could be caught if they escaped.

There is some disagreement about how severe the Puritans were in their daily habits. They could not gamble, dance or work on the Sabbath. Punishments were harsh. On the other hand, there were celebrations and children's games and toys. Although their wills were supposed to be broken, children were also valued.

We hear every Thanksgiving that the Pilgrims came to establish freedom of religion. Actually they came to establish their own religion, and were intolerant of others like Quakers or nonbelievers, especially in times of stress. Those who were not members of the Congregation, like the Carriers, were more likely to be accused as witches.

Many stresses hit Andover in 1692, with a torrential rain that washed out the early planting, followed by a drought. The fear of famine no doubt played a role in the witchcraft hysteria. Some attribute the craze directly to the eating of stores of moldy rye, contaminated with ergot, which can cause mania. This explanation ignores the social causes, and the fact that in England at the same time there were also executions of large numbers of witches.

One of the prime causes in Andover was the conflict between the Reverend Thomas Barnard and Reverend Francis Dane. Ten years before our story, Andover asked for a new minister, Reverend Barnard, because Francis Dane was so old. Reverend Dane, however, refused to step down, and the two men continued to serve together with a great deal of friction. Reverend Barnard had expected a full salary, and instead the salary was divided. Both men had to supplement their income, Dane with a school and Barnard by hiring women to weave and then selling their output. Although the witchcraft conflict could have been a cold-blooded attempt by Barnard to get rid of Dane by accusing all his relatives, it is more likely that Barnard believed that Dane was involved in witchcraft and should be brought down.

The fact that Barnard was the disciple of the famous Cotton Mather surely played a part. Mather made the actual statement in the story about witchcraft and about Martha Carrier ("an arrant nag who shall be Queen of Hell"). The description of the hangings of Carrier and the others, with the role of Mather in reversing the crowd sentiment, is taken from contemporary reports. Martha Carrier was indeed plain spoken, and made the statement quoted that she should "stick to Benjamin Abbott like bark to a tree" to prevent him taking the land she felt was hers. Her sons were as described in the story: tied neck and heels together till they bled from the nose and confessed. Martha herself, a brave and stubborn woman, never confessed, and she hung for it.

Gretchen Gibbs grew up in a small town in Massachusetts about forty miles from Andover, where her book takes place. When she discovered that her ancestors played a major role in the witch trials in Andover, she had to write the story. She created the diary of a real girl, her ancestor Maggie Bradstreet.

Gretchen is a psychologist who taught, practiced and conducted research for many years. She has published books and articles in psychology as well as short stories, memoir, and poetry.

48

$$12\overline{)144}$$
$$x\ 3$$

while

Charlie - Skyline

Wm 542-7978

cell: i'm hds

↗ ↙